Books by Bette Pesetsky

Confessions
of a Bad Girl

Confessions of a Bad Girl

Bette Pesetsky

ATHENEUM
New York
1989

Some of the stories in this book have previously appeared in
The Ontario Review, Canto, The New Yorker, The Paris Review, and *Vanity Fair.*

ATHENEUM
Macmillan Publishing Company
866 Third Avenue, New York, N.Y. 10022
Collier Macmillan Canada, Inc.

Library of Congress Cataloging-in-Publication Data
Pesetsky, Bette, ———
Confessions of a bad girl / Bette Pesetsky.
p. cm.
ISBN 0-689-12021-4
I. Title.
PS3566.E738C6   1989
813'.54—dc 19   88-39290
CIP

Designed by Erich Hobbing

10 9 8 7 6 5 4 3 2 1

Printed in the United States of America

For Irwin

Contents

~~~~~~

Confessions

Bad Girl

Confessions

Foul Play

~~~~~~

I consider myself a city woman—just as I have always considered myself a city child. My brother Sylvester speaks of himself as a country boy. Not true. Never mind that he wore overalls and thick work boots with metal tips. We were city children, raised by city parents, and ours were the stealthy ways of the city. That's what counts. How could we be country children when our town was forty-five minutes from the city. And when those miles between town and city would soon be filled with people and the town itself cease to be. City people living where winters were cold and winter days short and grey. What was I doing? Biding my time. The war was over. I was a scholarship student at the extension division of the state university. What a surprise that was to some people. With her sassy mouth, they said.

I was twenty that chilly spring of 1954 when my chance came—courtesy of Roberta. I met her when we sat side by side in a lecture hall, it was chance. We came late three times a week to Professor Usher's popular class in world history. Like the final reel of a Charlie Chaplin film, we pushed past feet, abandoned scarves, excused ourselves until we dropped into seats in the last row. Others already had notebooks open, pencils primed. Roberta and I missed the start of every battle—arriving when the soldiers were already reeling from the cannon.

Afterwards we left together, went someplace for a drink. Roberta drank rum and Coke. Roberta had ambitions. She said my hair was badly cut. Her mother had taken her to Chicago to have her nose done. Roberta was going to New York. Soon, she said. Want company? I asked. She shrugged. I'll introduce you to my friend Nathalie, I said. We'll both go. So I persuaded Nathalie. I was a good talker. Why not? I said. It's New York.

The snow had hardly melted when we celebrated friendship in an apartment on Twentieth Street. Even though I was the one who brought Nathalie and Roberta together, the fact that they hit it off, even became close, was irritating. But why shouldn't they? Pretty girls are alike, they are optimistic, they always have money. I on the other hand just got by.

Roberta and Nathalie planned to return to college in the fall, I kept my counsel. Only Roberta had a reason to be in the city—a bona fide member of the *Mademoiselle Magazine* College Board.

So we were in the city with Roberta getting all the attention and wearing plaid skirts that bounced around her knees and perfectly matched sweaters. Still, there was more to Roberta. Roberta was fun. Naked Roberta dancing around the apartment and shouting, "Skin, skin, my dears, is this year's look!"

We went to parties. Roberta took us everyplace. She was generous.

But one day that fashion season ended, and Roberta packed her suitcases with those new clothes. Home time, she said. No one listened. I knew what I had planned. I never guessed about Nathalie. Nathalie—that childhood friend—was also going elsewhere. She was loaded with secrets. The man, for instance. The one with the wife and the children. Just whispers overheard from the hall. "All right," Nathalie would say, "all right. I don't care, you know. You know I don't care." Later came those abrupt telephone calls to her father now remarried. The mother perhaps turning over in her grave. In the end Roberta, Nathalie, and I kissed and hugged each other. Good-bye, we said.

I could type. I found a variety of short-term jobs. Two years of college, I wrote on each application, 50 wpm, no experience. Why take chances? Any possible references wouldn't have been good.

I moved into a two-room apartment on West Tenth and ruthlessly pursued the friends whom Roberta had left behind. Maybe they couldn't remember which one I was. Sure, they would say, when I called, come over on Saturday. So I did, and no matter what the occasion I showed up with a pot, a bowl, a tray. Specialty of the day, I would announce, presenting the unwanted. *Bigos* rich with sausage, smelling of sauerkraut. A green-toned apple pudding for the Feast of the Harvest. Wait until you taste this! And I would drop a tray overloaded with crumbly babkas in the middle of a glass-topped coffee table— bombarding the air with a blast of poppy seeds.

Everything was planned, my gaudiness, the tight slacks, the presumptions. My looks were not in fashion. "I'm from a godawful place in the snowy depths of Wisconsin," I would say, about to shed, the listener thought, my private self. People like to hear about desperate conditions. This is how you behave when you are not pretty. Who would want to know me? But I had the advantage, you see, of having been poor. None of those people were poor. Maybe their parents had been without money, but they kept their mouths shut, those parents did. So I had that advantage and could plump myself down in the corner of someone's apartment and slowly peel away the romance of poverty. Guess what my best friend became? A prostitute, not a call girl, no, a genuine streetwalker, a classic lady of the night. I exaggerated. Veronica of the lustful appetites had never been my best friend.

If they looked away, if attention faltered as I put out details of a ragtag childhood, I would give them my very best fact. My father, I would say, ran away, deserted his wife and two babies—Huck Finn in reverse—and joined a circus.

In one of those rooms I met Barry. This is Cissie, the hostess said, sighing. Barry nodded. Could I tell that I was his type? I think so. He was truly fond of second-hand poverty. He called me his Princess Scheherazade. He told me right off about a girl named Sonia whom he had known forever and ever. And in return I told him that my parents had been Socialists but were now lapsed and that Daddy had been in a circus and about the circus poster that hung on the wall of my room. Barry said that he would like to see it.

Sometimes we made love on cushions tumbled on the floor and sometimes we did it right on the bed. Later we would sit Indian-fashion on the mattress and eat the food Barry brought over. Strange food to eat in that way. Cold broiled steak with wilting salads, chicken pot pies. I never reheated anything, and Barry never mentioned it.

＊　　　＊　　　＊

One evening the telephone rang. It was my mother.
"Are you all right?" Leah asked. "Doing okay?"
'Yes indeed," I said. "I've got a swell job, doing great."
"Keep in touch," Leah said. "George sends his love."
"Give George mine."

"My mother," I said, and bounced on the bed. We were sitting up, the sheet as tablecloth, eating lamb chops and broccoli, our forks coated with congealed fat.
"Really," Barry said with interest. "She's the one who lives with that man?"
"Yes, with George. And Daddy lives with Dorothy."
"And how do you feel about them?"
"Who?"
"Dorothy and George."
"Nice people," I said.

One day in November, Barry dropped his wallet on the table and I flipped through his celluloid-covered treasures. "Hey," I said, stopping at one picture. How did I know? She looked right. "Sonia?"
Barry nuzzled my neck, whiskers against soft flesh. "That's Sonia," he said.
Sonia in the photograph wore a summer dress, long full skirt, she had a single flower in her hand—picked from her garden?—and her hair was held back by a velvet band.
"Liberty of London print," I said. "Delman pumps."
That was training by Roberta.

When Barry came into the bedroom, I was posed. A red dress with black leopard spots, arms folded across my chest, a blue plastic rose popping up between my splayed fingers, hair pulled back by my velvet band.

"Very funny," Barry said. "Did you buy that stuff?"

Did he think I was crazy? I owned the dress. The flower too. But I bought the velvet ribbon from Lamston's.

"Owned everything," I said. I scratched my arms. The dress had elasticized bands on the sleeves.

I thought my rooms, home of my circus poster, were comfortable. Still, I felt everything was temporary. I suppose that was because I believed I was better than the surroundings. You could sink into either of my two canvas butterfly chairs, read under the sly light from a metal pole lamp, and beneath your feet were two grey rugs, easy to fold, without backing. The rugs were puppies in their season of shedding. "Deny you were here," I whispered to Barry, pretending to blow the veins of grey threads from his coat, his pants, his hair. Was he amused? Later he bought three whisk brooms with different capabilities, which he hung from hooks in the bathroom. Also he would make loops of Scotch tape and run them up and down his pants legs.

The circus poster, twenty-three by twenty-seven inches framed in solid oak, hung on the one long wall in my living room. Not a copy—an authentic poster advertising the 1870 Grand Tour of the W.C. Coup Circus. My father, I would say disdainfully. My father was in the circus. Not this one—another circus. I would give a poster tour—the wire walker, the liberty horses, the clown entree.

Barry loved the circus story. "Your father actually deserted you," he said, "abandoned you and your mother and your brother. Ran away and joined a circus."

"He came back," I said. "He was only gone fifteen months. What's fifteen months?"

"Nevertheless," Barry insisted. "Desertion is desertion."

Barry took me to see my first circus. I didn't want to go. "Circuses are for children," I said. "I'll wait until I have children."

"Nonsense," Barry said. "When you take children anywhere, you can't enjoy yourself. Kids are a pain. Watch the parents. Listen to them. They ask worried questions of the child—Do *you* like it?"

The circus was at Madison Square Garden. No tent. Still, I had a good time. A handsome man named Rudolpho did the high-wire act. The program said that Rudolpho's family had been aerial artistes for five generations. I whispered to Barry, "When I was a kid I thought my father was a performer on the trapeze."

In the shower, Barry scrubbed my back with a loofah. My hair, always wiry, was particularly bad after it was washed. Barry applied shampoo. He pushed his fingers into the suds. "My nest," he said.

Barry never got enough of my childhood, he was nostalgic for it. The father who ran away, the mother whom he falsely labeled absentminded, the aunt who smelled like—"What did you say?" he asked me. "Like the bottom of a purse," I said, giving Aunt Beulah a scent—a mixture of spilled Max Factor powder, scraps of paper, a stirring of crumbs. Barry cherished my youth, all of it—the suppers of oatmeal, newspapers pinned inside coats for warmth, trips to the butcher for chopped meat because the old goat liked to look at little girls and stroke their hair—but nothing serious.

Barry wanted my town too. Drive-ins? he asked. Sure, I replied. An A & W? Yes, I would say. Texaco stations? Definitely, I said. How long had I lived there? Long enough, I told Barry. It is all a suburb now, I said. Developments named Shady Haven, Happy Hollow, Gardenville. The miles are gone—those few miles between town and city, old miles once filled with three-cow dairy farms, with posted land, and the paper box factory. The telephone company stuck a building out there one year. "Where?" my mother would say and answer. "Why between nowhere and nowhere."

"I can imagine what it must have been like for you," Barry said, "when your father ran off. What kind of child were you then?"

I smiled. "A brat, I think."

These are the brat stories I told.

1. In the playing field behind the Second Avenue School located right on Fon Nur Avenue, three girls were involved in their favorite game—the one invented by Cissie. Two of the girls were nine, Cissie was seven. She had skipped two grades, and she was accepted because of her game and her daring. The game was called Imitations and the rules were rigid.

Elizabeth was taking her turn. "Do it there!" she said. "Do it there! Do it there!" The intonation was right, the breathy tone, the emphasis. Cissie and Nathalie and Elizabeth laughed, roared, doubling over until foreheads touched knees. Veronica's mother. And although they had heard the imitation dozens of time, the pleasure remained. "Mine!" Nathalie shouted. "My turn."

Their repertoire was limited, each girl having only a few imitations. Cissie's rules forbade the sounds of famous people, no easy movie stars, only neighborhood noises were eligible. Just the overheard.

"Drunken fool," Nathalie said, pinching her nose to create a high-pitched whine. "Slobbering bastard. Try coming near me! Just try!"

The girls smiled at each other. Their eyes shone with life and meanness. What a great game! They stretched and arched their necks.

Cissie took a deep breath. Male voices were harder, the skill needed greater. "Thought he had me by the balls, did he. I fixed him. Turned his back on me, and I let him have it."

The girls sighed. They stood up, linked arms, and kicked clouds of dust as they skipped across the field. It was Saturday morning. In a half hour the boys would arrive to play ball. No girl in her right mind would risk being found on the field. At the far end where the dirt turned into sidewalk, the girls solemnly kissed each other's cheeks. "See you at two," they said.

2. How they landed in Wisconsin. They crowded into Beulah's house. One week, Joe said. That's all I can stand that sister of yours. Leah paid no attention. She could sit right down, do her nails, open a book, read a magazine. It was her nature. Beulah on the other hand had summer covers on her chairs, a set of good dishes, and one framed picture from Woolworth's on each wall. Based on the appearance of each woman, the opposite would have been expected.

Beulah was a short, square-shaped woman with the kind of loose flesh that made you think of bedclothes, of stains, of stale air. When she felt the need for conversation, she gathered Cissie into her lap. Cissie could wiggle all she wanted, she was trapped. Be still, Aunt Beulah ordered. But soon Cissie forgot the babyishness of being held and listened. Beulah whispered about lovers not forgotten, about three husbands gone who knew where, about the pale green of Baltic grass at twilight, about the heavy scents of forbidden holidays, and the Slowacki line that began *Oh sweet nights of Poland . . .*

Cissie's favorite tale was about the very first man Beulah had ever loved.

"Who was your first lover?" Cissie would ask.

"A tall boy, a big man, back in Lublin."

Cissie nodded.

"A fine person," Beulah said, "named Tomasz, but thin-skinned—a man who couldn't take the sun—peeled like a scraped carrot. He was some kisser. Shy, his family said. What did they know? His mother wouldn't let him have me. So he married a bit of a thing. What happened then? That wife had a baby with three eyes."

Cissie shivered with ritual anticipation. "Three eyes? Where?"

Beulah touched her own eyes. "Here and here." Then she placed a finger right in the middle of Cissie's forehead. "And *here*."

Cissie was extraordinarily happy.

3. It was evening, probably summer. Didn't bugs beg for death as they bumped against the screen? In Beulah's house, Leah and Joe are dancing. The radio plays music from the Palmer House in Chicago. Joe is not joking. He is really dancing, his arms encircling Leah's waist. Leah moving so gracefully, it makes you hold your breath. Joe

hums, low deep sounds. Cissie watches from the hall. Across the room, in the doorway that leads to the kitchen, Beulah watches too. Afterwards, this seems to be such an unlikely activity that Cissie believes she imagined it.

Why did they leave Beulah's house? A family argument. Happened in the afternoon. Cissie was in school. The details concerned who had sacrificed what. We're out, Joe said. Just like that he rents four rooms on Twenty-eighth Street. Of these short blocks radiating off the Avenue, none had names except Tenell Place and that was barely an alley. Cissie wrote *Twenty-eighth* on the top of a sheet of paper. It looked terrible. "Imagine that printed on stationery," she said to Beulah.

Beulah shrugged. "Who do you have to write to anyway?"

4. "The word," Cissie told Elizabeth, "is *horse*."

The girls nudged each other. Who else should be let in? Cissie thought this over. Be clever, she decided. She let in Nathalie and Veronica. So they went around together, arms wound around each other's waists. "Today," they would announce, "is horse."

"Where's horse?" Or,

"Here comes horse."

"Be a nice horse," they would warn each other.

The truth of the matter was that once the word wound itself into Cissie's mind like a name tape with the letters repeated every few inches she became impossible, insolent, irritating.

Still, it was Elizabeth who went too far. Accompanying Cissie into the butcher shop, she told the butcher, "I'll have horse today." The butcher's face turned red. The girls ran, giggling and frightened. Their hard bodies collided.

And the butcher, an old man and intolerant, told Cissie's mother. He had only recognized Cissie. "What did she say? *Horse meat,* did she say?"

It was at this point that Leah was forced to act. She would not have bothered. The rolling minds of children, she often said. But now it was too much, four times at supper, once before washing up. At no time heeding the warning to stop, to be still, to shut up.

Leah took Cissie firmly by the arm and pulled her outside on the porch. Now, she said, pay attention. You say *horse* once more—never mind what the sentence—and you will suffer for it. Cissie stared at her mother. Leah looked threatening. Hadn't Beulah described beatings in Poland, the ones with a whip—the moans, the flow of blood, the mysterious graves beneath the branches of the silver ash?

5. What was horse? Horse was two naked boys galloping around the field behind the Second Avenue School. Boys stripped of their clothes by Theresa's brother recently sent home from the state farm school for delinquent boys in Oshkosh and the two Beckett brothers with dark destinies predicted. No one knew what had brought on the stripping. But suddenly came a whooping holler from the playing field during Boys' Gym. The sound erupting like a bomb in the middle of the once-a-week Mixed Grades Sewing Class taught by Mrs. Mellon. None of the girls thought much of Mrs. Mellon's brains, but they regarded her as a genuine object of curiosity, the only female teacher in the school who was married. Never mind the world of mothers. They stared at that teacher. Did she do *it*?

The day of the stripping, the girls were filling up small squares of torn-up bed sheets with sample stitches. "The

French stitch," Mrs. Mellon said and demonstrated. The older girls grinned. "The *Fre-ench* stitch," they said and made kissing motions when Mrs. Mellon turned her back.

The noise from the playing field grew louder. It sounded promising. The girls discarded their bits of cloth. Spools rolled dangerously across the floor. Suddenly all the girls were at the windows.

"Back!" Mrs. Mellon demanded. But she could not keep order.

Everyone pressed against the glass, until the biggest girls opened the three windows. "Look! Look!" they shouted, leaning far out. For a moment Cissie managed to push forward. Beneath the window two naked boys ran around the field, chased by their depantsers, who slapped at them with belts, buckles forward, forcing them on. "*Wee-wee*," the girls yelled. Cissie lost her spot at the windowsill, forced back by the stronger. She jumped up and down, balancing herself briefly by pressing her hands on the shoulders of those in front. She saw the boys always retreating, knees high, a steady gait. Two white horses.

6. When Cissie was ten she acquired this great gift. It came to her at the time when her family lived no more than two blocks from Fon Nur Avenue. Tacky street, Leah said. Cissie could have lived there forever—the street where she came into her own. It would always be *her* neighborhood. On an August day with the pure glow of shimmering yellow light that brings on migraines in those inclined, Cissie sat on the top step of Mrs. Schweiker's front porch, tucked her skirt between her legs, and said, "I see a tall man coming through your doorway. A tall blond man with a mustache."

Mrs. Schweiker leaned forward in her chair, peeling her damp back like a stamp from the chintz-covered cushion. "Yes," she said in a throaty whisper. "What else?"

"That's all," Cissie said, her vision had been bribed with lemonade, and it was sour. She put the half-filled glass down on the porch step where it was immediately circled by a widening sweat ring, then she jumped down the three porch steps in one leap, and walked across Fon Nur Avenue.

One week later a tall man with blond hair and a mustache marched through Mrs. Schweiker's doorway. He was her brother Manfred, unseen for two years—and he never before had a mustache. "Now," Mrs. Schweiker said to her neighbors, "is that the gift or isn't it?"

Mrs. Liverfreund who lived two houses away identified what Cissie had. "Second sight," the old woman said. "My Aunt Vera had it in Breslau. She could tell your death to the minute, everyone said. And weddings and illnesses. Told a woman that her baby would be born without feet and it was."

"Fools," Leah said when she heard about Cissie's new talent. "Who would believe that grown women could be such fools? Superstitions are invented to keep people down, turn their eyes from the truth—spiritualism, Ouija boards, fortune-telling—all designed to keep people down. A damp bit of paper on the forehead cures hiccups. Urinate on your hands and drive away a headache. Second sight!"

But then Leah was always thought to be eccentric. She read only books, and in two languages.

After the triumph of Mrs. Schweiker's brother, Cissie foretold the arrival of Anna DeGustus's frowning bridegroom.

What happened afterwards should not have been laid at Cissie's door. Still, every time she saw Cissie, Anna DeGustus shouted, *Dirty Gypsy!*

Then came a ruffle of second sightings—a grandmother going, the Toleicz boys shoving a man, the shoemaker moving. But the results of second sight didn't necessarily happen at once. Take the case of Abba Tiller. Cissie saw him appearing in his living room and surprising a stranger dressed in blue. But weeks went by and then months. Still, in late spring he came home unexpectedly and caught that wife of his.

Cissie never saw anything about her family. You better not, Leah warned. But second sight does what it wants. One Saturday, past six in the evening, Leah had just shoved the dinner dishes to the middle of the table, making a forest clearing complete with crumbs—when it happened. Leah kept on lettering a sign ruler-straight with the skill of her seamstress hands. *Join the Union,* she printed. Joe, sitting next to her, was drinking a cup of coffee.

Cissie never had any warnings—no prodromes, no sparkle of light, not even a movie fadeout. Suddenly Joe was walking through the doorway, moving with care, being quiet. The daylight was a blue-grey, the air was thin, somebody was hammering. Joe wore a pale yellow shirt, a black-and-yellow plaid tie, his black felt hat, and his good brown shoes with the perforated tips.

Cissie knew what to do when she wanted to get rid of a vision from second sight. It was blinking. Quickly she closed her eyes, then opened her eyes. It worked.

Joe was back at the table, putting down his cup, unfolding his newspaper. Cissie coughed, held her breath, let it out.

*　　　*　　　*

7. Beulah screams at Joe. Wastrel! Wastrel! This happens because Leah is sitting in a chair looking sick from what Cissie didn't know. Get out of here! Joe yells back at Beulah.

It was September, a month of crackling dryness. Possibly Joe hit Leah. Maybe it wasn't a smack, maybe it was a push. His hand had moved swiftly, short white fingers glazed with black hair. At any rate Leah was sliding on the linoleum, stopping finally with her shoulder jammed against a baseboard. What happened? She found handholds in the cracks of that ancient flooring, never mind the dress binding her white thighs. She was back on her feet. She grabbed a kitchen chair and held it in front of her, pointing the four legs at Joe. You come near me, she said, and I'll bash your skull in.

Later Leah twists herself in front of the mirror, her slip up and bunched across her shoulders. Her back has three large spreading bruises like Fourth of July rockets, dark purple in the center and pale mustard-color outward. Creeping bastard, she mutters. Creeping, rotten bastard.

8. When second sight came true, Cissie went up to Sylvester. Joe had vanished. After all, in the beginning, anything could have happened. "Foul play," Cissie said. "I think there has been foul play."

"I'll foul play you," Sylvester said and grabbed her arm.

Leah put cheese, bread, slices of dark garlicky sausage on the table. She poured milk into two glasses and stirred into each a generous tablespoon of Horlick's powder. "Consider," she said, "I am still here. I have not left you. What would you like to do?" she said. "Want to go to the lake for a swim?"

While Leah was talking to Sylvester and Cissie, Beulah was nervously pinching her own arms. "Be sensible," she said. "Don't lie to the children. Don't let them think that everything is the same."

"The same? Did I mention the same?"

Cissie thought that perhaps a cold rain might fall. But no, it was egg-frying weather.

The neighbors had a good time. Something on the side, Beulah whispered. Joe must have had something on the side. Cissie needed no explanation. Beulah had long ago told her about something on the side in the story about the man named Judmilla. He had something on the side. That was black-haired Morna. The niece of his own wife. But Leah had no nieces. So the something on the side had to be someone else.

Then what happened to Joe was solved.

"Guess where Joe is?" Leah said. She was talking to Beulah. She had a postcard in her hand. "Might as well give up right away," she sang out. "You'll never guess. Joe joined a circus!"

Leah collapsed in a chair, holding her sides as she laughed. "Joe," she said hysterically, "has joined a circus. In the middle ring!" she roared. "On a flying trapeze!"

Cissie saw him. She didn't have to close her eyes. It was Joe swinging through the air, wearing white satin tights, a cape sparkling with sequin stars.

"That's what he does," she told Sylvester. "He's on a trapeze."

"You bet," Sylvester said. "Our old man is the original man on the flying trapeze!"

*   *   *

What do you think?" Cissie asked Beulah.

She shrugged. "In Poland," she said, "they knew about circuses. Here—like carnivals, traveling piles of creaking ferris wheels and fat ladies and four-legged chickens."

That took the wind out of Cissie, but then she went to the library. Beulah was wrong. Joe could easily have joined a *real* circus. The library had books with illustrations from all the best ones—Barnum & Bailey, Sparks Circus, Downie Bros. Big Wild Animal Circus, The Mighty Haag Circus, Ringling Bros., Wheeler & Sautelle Circus. Joe's circus was called Carlyle's Three Rings, it wasn't in any of the books.

Cissie never claimed to foretell the future. She never knew that Joe was coming back. She opened the door one afternoon and smelled the festive odors of celebration. The surprise always was that Leah was a good cook. Leah could stand at the stove and cook when she wanted to.

Joe sat stiffly at the table, Joe in shirt and necktie. Did he look different? He looked the same. Cissie looked different, though. Sylvester and Cissie were children, and moved through time and were instantly changed. Cissie wasn't angry. She didn't want to yell, or hit Joe, or run away. There was a moment when she thought that Joe held out his hand. Did he expect to shake her hand? But she was a child, her hand was never shaken. She hugged her father as she had always hugged him, and he hugged back.

The conversation between Leah and Joe was soft and steady. Cissie wanted to break in, wanted to interrupt. They sat down to dinner. She grabbed her chance. "How was the circus?" Cissie asked.

Her father cleared his throat. "All right," he said.

≈≈≈≈≈≈≈≈≈≈≈≈≈≈≈≈≈≈≈≈≈≈≈≈≈≈≈≈≈≈

*   *   *

"I'm satisfied," Barry said, putting down his chopsticks. Barry was celebrating his birthday. Sonia was throwing him a party. "Be back," he said, "by two at the latest." He squeezed the last of his packet of soy sauce on top of his rice.

I thought of another tale to tell Barry. Too late—let Sonia tell him one. I ate some more cold shredded chicken and garlic sauce, then I cleared the plates from the bed. I put on my black slacks, my black sweater, my fringed yellow shawl, and I went to a party given by an acquaintance of Roberta's named Martha. I didn't go empty-handed, I brought a tray of pirogi, the potato and onion kind.

In a corner of Martha's kitchen I met Raoul eating my pirogi, picking up the cold slippery dough with his fingers. "Good," he said.

Raoul was studying economics. He was twenty-three. "I'm a graduate student," he said. He took off every second year and worked. He envied people who had the G.I. Bill. He had a half-time assistantship in Iowa. He was returning in the fall.

I took Raoul to my apartment to see the circus poster. I bolted the door. "If someone knocks," I said, "ignore the sound."

Later I told Raoul my stories and he asked me what had become of those people. Nathalie and Roberta were lost to me. But it was true that Veronica was a prostitute. Elizabeth had married. I said that my mother lived with a short heavyset man named George who sold paint or managed a paint store. He made my mother happy, and I thought they read out loud to each other. My father was married to Dorothy who had given up her Church for him. They too were happy. Sylvester had grown up and nothing bad had happened to him.

By the time August left its mark, Raoul and I were ready to be married.

I put an advertisement in the local newspaper—*Everything Must Go*. No telephone number, just my address and the date of the sale. The old woman who lived on the ground floor waved the newspaper in my face as I was unlocking my mailbox.

"Crazy," the woman said. "You never know who will show up."

"I'll take a chance," I said and started up the stairs.

"Two girls," the old woman called after me, "next block, chopped to pieces, both of them!"

Only ordinary people came to my sale. They didn't care what they said. Look at this! Imagine living with that! What a color! They poked at folded drapes. Then they bought everything—leaving behind only the detritus of my living, unfit for purchase: wire hangers bearing shreds of paper from the cleaners; the china water bowl from the cat that had escaped over the window grille one afternoon impaling only a fleshy ribbon; miniature paper parasols from drinks named Singapore Slings and Plum Delites. Also, magazines with important items marked by turned-down corners, a blue plastic rose, and fat envelopes fringed with scraps of paper. The rooms became bigger, dumb in emptiness.

The only possession worth money was the circus poster. I had tried selling it myself, but no takers. Not one decent offer. Just admiration from purchasers of secondhand canvas chairs.

Nothing to do but wrap the poster in brown paper and carry it to the dealer who had said a week earlier that he would buy it for three hundred. The check he gave me was fifty dollars short. The economy is declining, he said. I could have refused, but the frame was heavy, the hour was late, and the money was in hand.

I argued with Raoul. Our voices were loud and hostile. What was behind the quarrel? Raoul had looked at the boxes stacked to be shipped. The empty boxes still to be filled with what I had held back from the sale—locked in the bedroom, kept safe from buyers. "What's this?" he said. "And these? Why are you keeping this junk!" His leg, a thick athlete's leg, shot out, and he kicked a pile of books. Covers parted as they tumbled down. "Do you know how much money shipping *this* will cost!" he shouted.

"I want everything!" I yelled back.

And Raoul left the apartment, slammed the door.

It was true some of the items originally intended for the sale I had pulled back—odd dishes, meat-red plates circled with white, three shelves held together by a scrollwork of wrought iron. Not for sale, I had said. You can't have those. Thus, I retained a wooden milking stool, a grey chenille bedspread, a Christmas wreath made of pinecones.

I never doubted that Raoul would return and prepare those boxes for shipping. But alone in that apartment I sipped from a nearly empty bottle of vodka. In the living room was the long white wall with its whiter square where the circus poster had hung. I blinked my eyes. The poster did not reappear.

Any second sight had vanished long ago. My fascinated lovers. Did you *really* see those events, Cissie? Are you absolutely certain you saw them before they happened? Yes, I always said. I swear, I always said. When lovers became more permanent, they were less indulgent. For God's sake, don't tell that story, they said. Makes you sound crazy—soused, nuts.

Raoul came back, he used his key to the apartment. The uncovered windows framed a transparent blackness. I was squatting as I filled empty boxes, my back ached, my lips were chapped where I had sucked off the lipstick. I offered Raoul a roll of heavy twine and a knife to cut it, and he started to tie up boxes. I could see at once a hundred things that I could have left behind, but discarding was as much work as packing. There are limits to what you can do.

The Prince of Wales

My mother gave me a diary once—a small book with a puffy red leatherette cover, a lock, and a tiny gold key. Did you need a key? You could have opened that lock with a twist of a hairpin. I felt bad that I never wrote in that diary. I think my mother knew I never did. My mother also bought me the Nancy Drew books, she bought me *Black Beauty*, she bought me *The Little Prince*. My taste was for other stories, *real* stories. One day she found those I had hidden behind the refrigerator. She gave up on me. I became a sore spot to her. If that's the way you want to go, she said, go.

Someone would have to marry Fay. Howard bought a gun from a man beneath the railroad bridge. The Emmelins were planning to have his father put away. The Spaeckel boys went every Tuesday to a special house in Oconomowoc. When the kitchen shades were up, Mrs. Welch could be seen banging her head rhythmically against the wall.

And this was just one week's gossip.

※　　　　※　　　　※

It is true that my passion could have settled elsewhere. But you could transport gossip—gossip was at home anywhere. From 1949 to 1951 my family moved six times, fighting labor's battles from Milwaukee to West Allis to Sheboygen, then back again. Sometimes my family moved because some rubber-stomached landlady said, I don't want any more nuts like you living here—where do people like you come from anyway? Sometimes we fled the trail of bad luck—add to this the times when the furnace broke down or the doors slammed too hard if the rent was late. Back and forth, we went courting breakage with lamps and boxes tumbled into the trunks of ten year old cars.

We used to live on Twenty-first then off Twenty-ninth then on Twenty-sixth. The horizons of my life changed, but I always made friends.

Mine was a family of movers, searchers, mobile Americans. And I blamed a lot on that. I wasn't doing well in school. I said that was the reason, ignoring the fact that my brother received almost perfect grades. I said that what was solid in the world were tales. And so I found gossip, and it improved life.

Almost as soon as we settled into our new second-floor flat on Twenty-third Street, I met Gina Rheinhardt. I was fifteen and Gina Rheinhardt was twenty-eight. Gina had three children and her husband drove a Bluebell bus to Prairie du Chien and La Crosse and sometimes did the run to Duluth. Does age matter? Friends are friends. Coffee, Gina said. I was willing. Your mother? she added. I shook my head. Leah made her own coffee.

Gina's cups had names on them or sayings. I got a brown cup with *GIRL* in yellow raised letters with a bleeding glaze. Gina thought it was a Florida cup. All their cups were souvenirs, some from their trip to Florida, some from the mother-in-law in Santa Rosa and some from the Christmas Village in The Dells.

It's a dump around here, Gina told me. My family used to live on Twenty-fourth near the Second Avenue School, but I went to St. Anne's. I marched to that tune right through high school, and then I went into the telephone company with two of my girl friends. My Hugh was dating one of those girls, but she went to Chicago for a month and that was that. Hugh and I got married. I stayed on at the phone company for eight months until Dolores came. I was stuck then. After that, Sandy came, then Baby Hugh. I'd go back to the phone company in a flash, if I could.

Leah said that a woman that age taking up with me was bad taste. My mother didn't realize how snobbish she sounded. You would have thought we numbered people in our family who had amounted to something. I told my mother that she really didn't know Gina. Leah looked up from her book and said that she bet Gina Rheinhardt's table was sticky to the touch and in *her* bookcases were knickknacks and geegaws.

I didn't answer. After all, there were circumstances, I knew that Leah was touchy—especially now that she had a new job selling linens in Carpenter's Everything for Your Home, and they told her to wear dark dresses and they liked white collars. My mother hated pushing herself into a corset every morning. Hell of a way to live, she said. But she had run out of factory jobs. She was, she said, persona non grata in plenty of personnel offices. My father had a pinched nerve and pain that sizzled through him. It was verifiable. He brought home an X ray one day and dropped it on the table. See, he said. My father did what he could.

Gina and I traded movie magazines—we knew who were seen together, knew about mysterious liaisons, and unclaimed children. I supplied items from the newspapers. Whatever Gina missed, I filled in. Gina was not basically a reader, but she had imagination.

But Gina didn't have a sense of history. I tried to tell her how good gossip was in the past. In fact, how all the truly great stories seemed to be over. Hadn't everything really important happened before I was old enough to talk about it. Consider the Prince of Wales and Wally. That had everything—a *real* king. Charlie Chaplin and all those girls. Fatty Arbuckle. All before my time. You had to read about them. That's the problem, Gina said. That was all yesterday—that can't change. She was interested in what was happening now; after it was over, she was done with it.

I had developed a philosophy of gossip. I explained what it was one Saturday morning to Gina. Gossip, I said, is like fairy tales. Think about fairy tales. Take "Rumpelstiltskin" for instance, it's a scandal, isn't it, if that ugly old gnome gets his hands on that pretty young girl. Same with "The Snow Queen" and "The Princess and the Pea." That's fairy tales for you—a lot of wicked stepmothers and wrong marriages and mistreated children. We could do local fairy tales. When we saw Mr. Zimmerman drunk—pull that thought out further—make him come home every night nearly passed out, pissing on the stairs in front of everyone and Mrs. Zimmerman moaning that she shouldn't have married him and wished that he were dead. A fairy tale—the start of a fairy tale. Get it?

Gina stared at me, then she yelled at Baby Hugh to get away from the door, then the other two came in wanting cookies, and Big Hugh shouted from the bedroom that we must all shut up or he couldn't sleep.

So I had to be content with movie magazines and local tales. It's true that sometimes my Aunt Beulah, unasked, would read out loud her letters; they contained gossip, but who knew the people. Achbend's divorce, Tilmo's self-hatred, the explosive nature of Gottbaum. Leah might nod. But too many details were missing for me.

Even real gossip had to be changed sometimes. What's true isn't necessarily believed. For instance, one night I saw two people making love on the roof across the street. If they stayed on the flat part, I might not have seen them, but they spread a blanket on the slanted side. They were up there, most of their clothes off—body shadows with the moon in its fourth quarter and with the low orange glow from the street light. The man was more indistinct, but the woman I saw clearly. I knew both of them, man and woman. But who would believe the story— that I stood at the window of my own darkened bedroom bold as a lark and watched at ease. So I changed it, I stuck the man and woman in a car parked behind the school playground, had myself pass by, reporting that I saw only a glimpse, but any fool could tell what went on.

Still, gossip is fickle in the way it behaves. Take the best story to cross this neighborhood in years, and I wasn't the first to hear it. Never mind that the chief player was someone I knew. I knew her before she quit school. I have enough typing, Elizabeth said. Who needs more? I can make a living.

The story came from Gina. Gina, migrating one day from supermarket to laundry, heard the tale. You'll never, she said to me, never in a million years guess what I heard. You know Dora's daughter Elizabeth? Fat Elizabeth? I nodded. She is going to be married, Gina said. Guess who's the lucky man? Oh guess! I give up, I said. The butcher, Gina said triumphantly. *Your* old butcher. God, I said, and sucked in my breath. Yes, Gina said. I heard it myself this afternoon from her cousin. Elizabeth's got a ring already. How's that for news?

Leah said that the marriage-to-be was like a primitive sacrifice. Elizabeth—how old was she?—seventeen probably. And that ancient man. That old man past seventy. It was almost white slavery. She had half a mind to see Elizabeth's mother and tell her what was what. Maybe there was even a law. Don't you embarrass me, I said. You? Leah said. Then we were yelling, and afterwards I knew that the neighborhood had heard too much.

But Gina said the next morning, show me a family that says it doesn't fight and I'll show you liars. The reason I never heard her and Big Hugh, she said, was because their quarrels tended to occur mostly at nine or ten in the morning before Big Hugh went to bed. I was in school then.

How much did we know about Elizabeth and the butcher? I used to say that Elizabeth was left behind in everything. It was true. All the other girls slimmed down and grew tall. Elizabeth stayed as she was in eighth grade, short and squatty, with baby plumpness hardening into wrinkled permanence above her waistband.

On a Saturday two months before the wedding Gina and I planned an expedition past the butcher shop. Arm in arm and giggling, we walked down the street; her three children, bribed with candy, were circling us like a litter. Reconnoitering, we said, and nudged each other. The butcher behind his counter was visible from the window. Look at him, we whispered, pretending to be reading his specials. The old butcher—an ancient, withered man. It was reported that he had been in the infantry under the Kaiser. Anyway, the butcher came from Mannheim in 1935 or 1936. That's what someone remembered.

The butcher's meat wasn't anything wonderful, but he would cut to order, and sell little pieces. He made sausages too and sold a line of cheap cold cuts to fit the neighborhood. Leah said that she had never eaten stuff like that before and wasn't about to start now.

Did he like little girls? Yes, according to rumors. His mother lived with him for years. In summer children would yell in squeaky mimicry of her voice—*Oh Heinz, Heinz, wann machen wir Licht?* The bolder girls would pretend to be that old woman wandering through darkened rooms. They would bump into trees and bushes until their laughter made them stop. Gina said that Elizabeth would fit right into that family, like stuffing in one more prune. Imagine that one having fun! Gina said you could tell who were the prissy virgins. Look at their umbrellas, she said. They carry big, black, men's umbrellas. Why, she didn't know.

Inevitably, though, sex was going to happen to Elizabeth with that old man, his clothes off, bare and shivering. It was possible that the butcher had had many women before. Anything is possible. He had never seemed strange or shy. He could have had plenty of women. I rubbed my shoulders. Did an old man's hands slide down a girl's body with slow cautious caresses, the fingers tapping out an experienced beat like a rat-a-tat-tat. Baby, would the old man whisper, sweet sugar child. Maybe in German.

Anyway, Elizabeth would never tell me. I could understand how you would feel if it were some boy—someone trying to get you in the back of a car—someone saying, hey come on, come on, and pulling at your clothes.

I bought a box of note paper, pale blue, edged with a line of white. *Congratulations,* I wrote. *All the best happiness.* I had never written anything like that before. I tried saying the words out loud. They didn't sound that strange.

Was it the note that got me the invitation? Just to the reception. *Come Celebrate With Us* in raised gold letters on cream-colored paper. Some people have all the luck, Gina said and held up the invitation for the admiration of the six women in her kitchen. They were women from the neighborhood. They examined my invitation. Then it came out—who else was invited. Three, four of the women. The butcher's customers. Better customers than Gina, who stopped in once in a while for soup bones and a bit of ham. She was out in the cold. Well never mind, Gina said, secondhand is better than no hand. Cissie will tell the story.

Twice that week we all met in Gina's kitchen and explored the situation of Elizabeth and the old butcher. Her mother had watery eyes. The father was a drunkard. You'd think the Church would stop it. The selling of a child. What else was it? Sometimes as we spoke, the real Elizabeth vanished, she became tall and thin and blond and locked in a tower.

Leah was not pleased. It smells, she said. How did you get invited anyway? Let her go, my father said. What's the difference. It's life.

Leah stared at me. That better not be life. Don't tell me you and Elizabeth are still friends? she said.

Friendship is never lost, I replied.

Where were they holding the wedding reception? The butcher rented the Stinson S. Weaver Hall. I knew that hall—a red brick building with factory contours. I knew the cold touch of its smooth plaster walls against my back where I had stood and listened to the hiss of radiators as I handed out union literature to the almost-converted. I did that once a month until I got old enough to refuse. Do it yourself, I said.

For the reception I had to wear my green plaid school skirt and a white blouse, but I had decent stockings and new black shoes. I intended to see everything, a reporter from start to finish. But when I arrived at the hall, it was clear that I had missed a lot. Neighborhood men stood in the doorway drinking bottles of the butcher's beer, men laughing and making ominous noises, men sweating even in the chill of the dark night.

The hall was still itself despite the white crepe paper streamers and all the lights—it didn't look festive. That's why it was such a bargain to rent—for what it lacked.

Everyone I knew seemed different, though. All the neighborhood women became strangers. Dressing for a party had aged those women, given them guarded eyes as they sat in groups for their matronly monitoring, yelling that's enough to little children out there in the center of the floor who pretended to dance and bumped into every-one. Who was my age? The bride.

I followed the flow of people to a row of sawhorse tables covered with platters of food—grey to pink to rosy-red sausages mounded in magical pyramids, scoops of purple cabbage in puddles of lavender milk, pale strings of cole-slaw. I would skip the food. But a drink? No one paid any attention. I took a glass of beer.

People said hello and how are you doing, but no one asked me to sit down. I put my back against a wall. Anyway, I wasn't present to have a good time—I was there to observe.

It was a noisy wedding. Music from a three-man band on the low platform. Three old men—the one with the accordion standing in the middle. They played fast dance music and polkas. Guests shouted requests. Do *The Four-Eyed Beggar*! Play *Catherine's Crawl*! Everyone tapping, swaying, whistling.

At the far end of the hall Elizabeth's mother sat fanning herself with a paper napkin, her cheeks glowing, her mother's dress pink, her hair an upsweep of rolls and curls. The bride stood nearby in a white lace dress that stopped unreasonably above her fat ankles. The bridegroom was on the floor dancing first with this woman, then with that.

I finished my glass of beer, licked the streak of foam from the rim. I was trying to put it all in memory—who danced, who sat, who laughed—but each impression began to chew up the last until it was all crowd and music. Nothing to cling to. And later with Gina, there would be a quiz.

I saw Elizabeth. I could see her clearly. The bride standing alone by the platform. I ought to speak to her. Anyway, it would give me something to do.

Many congratulations, I said. Elizabeth smiled back, her lipstick smeared from too many kisses. She plucked impatiently at her bodice, wrinkled and snug against her body.

Want to see the rings? she said and held out her hand. Glass-bright glitter beneath my nose.

Much happiness, I said. They're gorgeous.

Elizabeth giggled, quickly looked around. His cousins, she whispered, are mad as hell.

The music rolled to a stop. Wait, Elizabeth said, her hand on my arm, and she called out to her butcher. You know Cissie, she said.

Ah, the butcher said. Come dance with me, Cissie.

Go on, Elizabeth said, encouraging me. I've slid my shoes off—be a half hour before I'll be able to get them back on.

I couldn't refuse. The butcher had me, he moved me, he twirled me. I hadn't seen him up close for years. In my thoughts I had given him rheumy eyes, coarsely shaven skin, hanging flesh. I spared him nothing. But the truth was that he didn't look so bad, not so old, not so fat. Had he been someone else once? His shoulders were straight and firm.

Dancing, he whispered to me, is an art. The secret is all in the concentration. He bounced me forward. He certainly had plenty of energy. How well did he know Elizabeth?

Round and round the butcher led me, and when the accordion signaled with crashing chord the end of that dance, the butcher bowed, not a courtly bow but a flashy Arthur Murray bow.

He had worn me out. I found an empty chair, my chest heaving and the sound of seashore waves in my ears. I focused on old landmarks—the blistering paint, the ceiling-crack, the striations in the third glass globe that swayed from its chain.

Where was the butcher? The butcher was back on the floor with someone wearing a long black velvet dress—a heavy-breasted woman, a genuine Valkyrie.

I was hungry. I went over to the tables and filled a plate with pink sausage and purple cabbage, added sharp mustard and a hunk of sour rye bread. How good it all tasted!

Toasts! It was a drinker's shout, immediately picked up by others. Toasts! Toasts! they chanted. Trays of glasses filled with wine were passed. I took a glass.

To the bride and groom! To happiness! To long life! To forever and forever!

The bride and groom were pushed forward. My father was right. This was life. I stood up on my chair, balancing carefully in my new shoes, my tiny heels. What did I see? I saw the butcher's hand move down Elizabeth's back, saw his fingers squeeze one buttock, pinching the lace dress, before moving upward. Bride and groom climbed the three steps leading to the platform. The band played a piece romantic with vibrato.

The butcher waved at the crowd with one arm as the other now curved across Elizabeth's shoulders and pulled her close. How fit the butcher seemed, how young, and Elizabeth standing next to him in her tight white dress, her curls still fresh from yesterday's perm, raised her hand in enthusiastic acknowledgment of all those good wishes.

The Spacedons

≈≈≈≈≈≈≈≈≈

I said that half of life is coincidences and the other half is
thought out and my mother looked up and said that's
right. That's the kind of mother she is. What I meant, I
think, is that it was coincidence how I became a member
of what the newspapers called a gang and that my leaving
was thought out. What happened is that on the playing
field just behind the school we were fooling around when
a kid named Appleton swung his arm and hit my jaw
where an aching tooth sang its own arias. Had he altered
his random motion, the arm would have connected with
my shoulder. And I would have done nothing. But the
shock of the pain dazzled my mind. He had sent something flying that must ricochet back. And I fell upon
Appleton. From my father I had learned this: the fight
with the bigger enemy cannot be fair—by its very nature,
it is unfair. Therefore, no rules. In my assault on Appleton, I gouged, I pulled, I plunged him through a repertoire of dirty blows. And when it was over, I was
surrounded by the admiration of Frank T. and what passed

for his gang. They slapped my back, mean small boys. I had brought Appleton down; he stood for something, and I had made him eat dirt. I beamed back. Thus, I moved from altruism and ignorance to a position of threat. I was dangerous. Nice kids avoided me.

The advantage of the group was immediate. For a while I basked in acceptance. It was the unvarying routine that made me long for the days before I destroyed Appleton. We were into petty crime. Frank was our leader. Over and over we performed the same acts of despair. It was not that Frank was afraid, only that he lacked imagination.

What I did was a thing so dumb that it put me out of the running forever. I took up juggling. Frank publicly named me El Freako.

Jugglers must have great lives. At one time I could juggle four oranges. I did this where anyone could see—usually at the edge of the woods north of the playing field. I would announce an act. "The Great Sylvester," I would say, "straight to you from the capitals of the world!" I could keep four oranges floating in the air and spinning. I thought that was a feat, a natural talent, believed that I was the only one who had thought of it. But one day two other boys appeared—younger. One with oranges, the other with apples. So it turned out that juggling fruit was not unusual. I went to cupcakes then, the kind you buy in cellophane packages, two to a package. I could keep five packages going. The packages were light, given to crushing, undependable in their flight. If I could keep all five packages in the air for one hundred spins, I could eat the cupcakes. It was a bargain with myself. That I could do this would have amazed plenty of people. Maybe if they didn't know me, they picked me for a team. But give me a regular ball and I dropped it. Couldn't keep my mind on it.

All that autumn I practiced being unnoticed. It was hard. I took up baking bread. Aunt Beulah breathing a cloud of flour in her kitchen taught me what she knew. My specialty was a particularly thick and crumbly brown bread. I found the recipe in a history book. *Panis sordidus.* My sister Cissie said, how you can be such a jerk. Everyone is talking about you. I told her to shut up or I would break her arm.

How did I find the Spacedons? I went looking for them. Those were the times when boys craved jobs after school— they respectfully delivered your groceries, mowed your lawn, were on the lookout for the stray errand to be done. So I walked down Twentieth Street, crossed the highway, and met the Spacedons.

I admired the Spacedons. They were truly out of it. I'll tell you what I know about true weirdos. True weirdos look like everyone else. People thought my family was the peculiar one in town when all the time it was the Spacedons. My family had normal values. Hidden maybe, but normal. For instance, Mrs. Hillcock called my sister Cissie a bitch. Then two days later, Mrs. Hillcock is walking down Twenty-sixth and past our house. My mother, the bookworm, gets up from the porch where she is reading. She walks down the path—not dressed like other mothers. She is wearing one of her pleated skirts and those white ankle socks of Cissie's. Easy as can be and not a word exchanged, she punches Mrs. Hillcock in the nose. Blood, that woman later declared, blood down the front of her dress, and swelling and cartilage damage.

Now, this incident was cited as the act of foreigners—but what you have is the normal instinct of the mother bear or tiger or perhaps even the ant. The defense of the young.

The Spacedons lived in a large house at the end of their street. My father said that if the building had been kept up, the property would have said money. But it sat like a chewed upright pencil on a wide lawn. One of those Space-don kids, my father said, could have tried a paintbrush.

Five Spacedons. A mother and two sons and two daughters. They all led adult lives, although between me and Donna were no more than three years. Every morning the Spacedons piled out of their house, climbed into a Buick, and went off to the city. They traded the Buick every two years—went from black to navy blue and then back to black. Weekdays about six in the evening, they returned. So they were not around all that much.

Everyone said they must be socking it away—but that was said with admiration as they had no reputation for tightness, just for caution. On Halloween the kids made a beeline for their house. Mrs. Spacedon always gave candy. But that didn't matter, no sooner had the kids collected and said their thank-yous and the door closed than they started soaping the garage windows, smashing eggs on the lawn, dribbling honey on the path.

I admired the Spacedons. William was getting ready to go off to war. Town girls said he was a heartthrob. Clement was the youngest son, and I liked him best. Too bad he wasn't a Catholic, the girls said. There was a man who would have had a vocation. What happened was that the war shipped William to Missouri, while Athena, the oldest girl, went off to Washington, D.C., to serve the country as a secretary. Clement and Donna stayed home with Mrs. Spacedon.

But when I first knew the Spacedons, they were all home. Clement was the one who hired me. We need, he said, someone to cut wood. Does your mother let you use an axe? You bet, I said, having never touched an axe in my life. My mother was theoretically opposed to the burning of wood indoors. My Aunt Beulah had stories about innocent babies who had been incinerated by a stray cinder.

I got Billy Beckett to show me how to handle an axe and use a wedge. Billy didn't mind, there wasn't much that he could teach. And in exchange, I showed him how to short the ignition wires on a car—something he should have figured out by himself.

My first Spacedon task was chopping up two spindly trees that had been on the ground since spring. I got splinters, a callused palm, and once came close to whacking off my thumb. But when I finished, I piled the pieces of wood against the side of the house. They made a satisfyingly high pile. Clement paid me. You're in business here, he said.

The Spacedons look like everyone else. Their difference is a secret. My family does not look like everyone else, we are a sharp-faced people, given to growing wild hair, and not outlandish dress but wrong—wrong colors, wrong for the time of year. My mother says that doesn't matter. My sister Cissie loves crazy colors. My father will wear a tie when no one else does and vice versa. The Spacedons always wear dark colors in winter, pale in summer. They have good manners. Hi and how are you, they say to everyone. My family carries grudges, sometimes not speaking to those we loathe, and we loathe often. Not the Spacedons—they are perfect models of propriety.

That's how I recognized what they were.

Mrs. Spacedon, all bones and sharp angles, liked to dig around the flowers, she was always bending and scratching at the soil. She wore print dresses in good weather and sounded when she spoke as if she were a Southern lady in the movies. South Chicago, my mother said scornfully. But Mrs. Spacedon treated me fine. If she was around when I was working—I had graduated from chopping wood to repairing the back porch—she would call out, Do you want something to drink, Sylvester?

She was willing to give me anything—ever beer. It didn't matter that I was fourteen. But I hadn't accepted my shortcomings yet, I was still thinking athlete. I never accepted the beer.

One Wednesday evening, the Spacedons came home and I was still outside working, never mind the icy wind, I was carefully piecing together a railing. I had sanded the wood to a silky glow. Mrs. Spacedon came outside. Freezing, she said. Stay and have supper with us, Sylvester. Wednesday is a good day—we have Spanish omelet and home fries and biscuits.

I accepted. I thought I would get a chance to see the rest of the house. I had never been past the kitchen and the small bathroom just off the porch. And I was curious about the Spacedons—about seeing them up close.

Mrs. Spacedon never said anything about calling my parents to find out if having me stay for supper was all right. And I knew that was stranger than the fact that I didn't have to go home. Taking nourishment, my mother always said, was an individual responsibility. You eat or you don't.

I hesitated in the doorway like a dusty laborer who should not pass the linoleum, doomed to eat standing in a corner of the kitchen. But the Spacedons didn't seem to care how I looked.

For goodness sakes, Donna said, don't be a statue in the middle of the floor. Am I supposed to walk around you? Go sit in the front room until the food is ready.

That loosened my feet. I went straight down the hallway. If my dust didn't bother them, well then it didn't bother me. I headed towards the rosiest glow. Most houses in town kept the lights off unless someone was in the room. Do you own stock in the electric company? Spacedons went around turning on lights.

The rosy glow of the light was caused by the lampshades—pink silk stretched on wire frames. Plenty of chairs and tables. Carved wood—rosettes, cherubs, scrolls. I knew that the Spacedons sold furniture. Somewhere in the city they were reported to have a store, Antiques—The Past for You. Should I sit down? Boy, would my father hate this room. He's a coffee splasher. And think about the soft black ink from the sports pages. I spread newspapers wide when I read—but our couch was kind of a dirty brown.

I became a semi-regular at the Spacedon's supper table. I tried their Tuesdays—spaghetti and meatballs. Monday was tuna casserole, which I could just as soon skip.

Mrs. Spacedon was a good cook. That was one of the things I learned. Appearance and good cooking aren't the same. You cannot tell from how a person looks whether the food will be worth eating. The Spacedons taught me about hot sauces. I copied the way they used them. First time, I poured on too much Tabasco. Fire in hell is what I said, when I tasted my eggs. William snickered. Donna too. We should have warned you, Mrs. Spacedon said. Takes a while before you can spice the way we do.

Most families, when they pair off, go with the oldest together and the same for the youngest. But the Spacedons were all adopted, so age hadn't much to do with it. They divided into Athena and Clement and then William and Donna. The first meal at their house, I remember how the Spacedons spoke to each other. Donna suddenly saying to Athena that her father must have been slow too. And Clement coming back with—at least *her* mother must have had manners. Then William saying it was too bad that Donna's mother wasn't pretty. I must have coughed at that. The Spacedons looked at me. We were just joking, Clement said.

Clement came first, he was the oldest in the family in time. Then Athena. They were the first brother and sister. Then came Donna, and last William. So the rank of brothers and sisters in the family had nothing to do with real age.

I talked about the Spacedons a lot. My mother took a dislike to them. They make jokes, I said, repeating conversations. They torment each other, my mother said.

No one actually mentioned Mr. Spacedon. Mr. Spacedon must be dead, I told my mother. She looked up from her book. Probably buried in the garden, she said.

In summer I weeded for the Spacedons. They had land both fertile and curiously untidy. Was it that the flowers did not match? Short among tall. Cross-pollination making its own. Work is a benefit, Mrs. Spacedon said. I told my mother. She snorted. Your work, she said. Not hers. My mother said that woman wasn't paying me enough to slave over her flowers. Twenty-five cents an hour!

*   *   *

The next year I didn't work for the Spacedons, although Mrs. Spacedon called me. I already had a new job in the paper box factory, working during the school year on Saturdays and every day during the summer. Paper boxes for war. It was the money. They paid good money. I had greater needs now. I had begun to take out girls. Still, from time to time I stopped by the Spacedon house. Mrs. Spacedon offered me fifty cents an hour. Come back, she begged.

When I graduated high school my mother and father took us to the city for a celebration at the Shroeder Hotel. First, my sister Cissie wouldn't go. But then my mother pinched her arm. She went. God, Cissie kept whispering in the car. I knew what she thought. She thought we would make fools of ourselves. I knew she was wrong. I could have told her that. We are not different, I would have said. Just wait.

I was right. We were seated in the hotel dining room, and my mother and father were acting as if we ate that way every day. Only Cissie hid her menu for a souvenir. Even when my father made a toast to me, no one turned around to look.

I went away to college, but the town didn't disappear from my life. Aunt Beulah cut out items from the newspaper and sent them to me in heavily stuffed envelopes. Thus, I learned that William Spacedon had moved to California, and that Athena had returned to her family from Washington, D.C. And one spring vacation, I was driving past the post office when I saw Clement. I waved at him, and he waved back.

*   *   *

I was going to a new life. I thought that—believed that the town and I were finally permanently parted. Then my father got sick. Don't worry, my mother wrote. Garden-variety surgery. At St. Clare's they removed his gallbladder, but afterwards a bacterial infection set in, and the fever would not go away. I left college in the middle of my junior year. My mother was angry. It's not necessary, she said.

My sister was still at home, still in school. My father was in bed. The doctor explained everything. Who can tell? the doctor said. Your father is not responding. Bed rest, the doctor said. Maybe bed rest.

So I went out to the paper box factory and they took me on. A few of the boys I had gone to high school with were there, we greeted one another. I was back, they thought. I had finished with whatever I had been doing, I had taken a job, I was an adult. I lost my student disguise. As long as I was at college, people would ask me what I was planning to be—surely my studies were intended to lead to a useful occupation. And how I answered depended on what I liked most that semester, but if I kept my reply practical, no one minded. That's nice, they would say.

One day my mother said, you'll get a laugh out of this. Mrs. Spacedon must have seen you in town. Would Sylvester like to do some work for them? she asked. Not my son, I said. Ten-cents-an-hour employer!

I drove over to the Spacedons' that evening and rang the doorbell. Mrs. Spacedon opened the door and immediately hugged me. Sylvester, she said. Look everybody, it's our Sylvester! Big boy now, she said, and winked. But not too big for some weeding—seventy-five cents an hour?

Clement shook my hand. She's getting old, he apologized.

They invited into the kitchen where we sat and ate bowls of hazelnut mocha ice cream. The Spacedons looked genuinely pleased to see me. Athena had grown pale and thin. Donna on the other hand had plumped and filled out—turned into a lively and pretty woman. She practiced flirting with me—probably because I was shy and wouldn't say much back. It was a pleasant evening. Come back soon, everyone said.

Clement called me a week later. Trouble with a car. Athena had purchased a secondhand car. No one else in the family knew about cars now that William wasn't home. I went over to help. Clement and Athena were hovering over the black Chevy—three, four years old. They looked as if they were trying to tell something from the finish of the paint. I thought they had been taken—the car was basically a lemon. I tinkered with the car all that winter—kept it going. That, my mother said, is poor use of your time. Do you know what mechanics get paid?

One Saturday morning, the hood was up, trouble was in the silence of the car. But mechanically there is still the unexpected. The motor roared. Athena and I smiled at each other and she blew me a kiss.

I invited her to the movies. The invitation came easily. I meant it as a symbol of friendship. That's what I meant. No shortage of girls in town. No pity involved. I was not in the mood to feel sorry for anyone except myself.

I came by to pick up Athena in an old, humpbacked Ford. Much worse-looking than her car except for the silken sound of its works. Athena waited for me on the porch. She looked nice. She was shorter than me. I thought she would be mistaken for an older sister. I suggested *Cyrano de Bergerac* with Jose Ferrer. Playing at the Savoy. I thought that was her kind of picture. Sounds fine, Athena said.

After the movie I took her to the Squire Inn for coffee and pie. What would I talk to her about? I was twenty. Easy enough to speak at the Spacedon table—enough people there. I stirred my coffee and sorted through possible topics—her car, adoption, Mrs. Spacedon. I chose Mrs. Spacedon.

How did you feel? I asked. The first time you met Mrs. Spacedon—your mother.

Athena put down her cup. It's not what anyone thinks—it was never like a foster home, she said sharply. Never mind that none of us were infants when we arrived. It is a home—with a true mother. And where would we have been without Mrs. Spacedon—Donna, Clement, William, and me?

I was upset. Athena's face was flushed. She was speaking seriously. I had no idea how to answer. Who spoke seriously? My mother was sarcastic, my father spoke to the clouds, Aunt Beulah to reminiscences. But Athena was speaking directly to me. I fell in love with her.

All of the reasons for being in love with an older woman, having an affair with her, are known—I acknowledge all of them. The very selfishness of such a relationship. Yet, this ignores the fact that Athena was a good person, an attentive lover. How gently she must have culled her memories to keep me from feeling awkward. Through the winter it was Athena and me. That I asked her to marry me is unforgivable. That I even allowed that thought to progress—the angry scene with my mother, my sister's scorn, Clement's silence. Still, I didn't stop anything. Athena planned a wedding, bought a dress. Sometimes I thought that only Mrs. Spacedon truly understood. My sweet girl, she said to Athena. My sweet girl is marrying. Love is love.

Yet all that time, didn't I know that I would pull back, that I would become frightened and wonder how this could possibly have happened.

In spring my father ventured out into the yard, his body wrapped in a rug from some boat, a steamer rug that seemed to be mysteriously part of our possessions. I feel like a new person, my father said. Truly a new person.

My father said that his dream of success had solidified. He would make it, he swore.

What does she look like? Aunt Beulah asks. This love of your life?

So I describe her.

Nice, I said. And pretty. Her skin is as soft and smooth as a girl's.

Aunt Beulah stands behind me and rubs my shoulders. Such marriages can work out, she says. Did I ever tell you about Shlomo and Rebecca?

Yes, I say, and flee the house.

My mother splutters questions. What will you do? Where will you live? In her house? With her crazy family? Will you work all your life in that factory on the highway behind those blue glazed windows with the spiderweb cracks?

*   *   *

It was difficult to say how the quarrel began or whether it was planned. It could have been no more than nerves, or hallucinations moving from dreams to daylight. And no one remembering afterwards. Was it about pancakes? Sugar? The length of a race? The name of a dog that a man named Martin once owned? Athena left my car and ran into her house. The shadow of Mrs. Spacedon appeared at the window. Was she spying on us? The old woman—the old witch—the old coot. I was angry, I was furious, my mouth filled with spittle and bitter flavors. I gave my notice at the factory the next day. Athena's wedding dress was packed away. I will never marry, I told my mother.

My mother shrugged. Maybe, she said. Wait a few years after the sharpness goes. First love. Who forgets first love?

My mother did not return Mrs. Spacedon's telephone calls. It was after you left, Cissie told me years later, it was then that Mrs. Spacedon came to the house. She must have walked, Cissie said. There was no car parked out front.

It would have been a long walk for an old lady. I could see that woman struggling against the wind, fearfully crossing the highway, the lights trigger-short. Let me in, let me in, Cissie reported. Over and over that woman called and hit against the door. All that time, Cissie said, our mother sat in the kitchen. No one, she ordered, goes near that door.

Athena married a man I never knew and went to live in Baltimore. An announcement of her wedding appeared in the local newspaper. Aunt Beulah sent the clipping to me. I think, that is wonderful. She is happy. I am happy.

❋   ❋   ❋

Have I spoken to others about Athena? When it comes to that point in a relationship—the recounting of old loves. The women always like to hear about Athena. A tale of melodrama and sadness, well suited to lost romance. Then too they never see Athena as a competitor.

I always speak about the family. The vapors of old Mrs. Spacedon floating around. I tell how good the Spacedons were, how they embraced me and made me feel one of them. I describe Athena as warm and loving—her kindness, her passion.

One day the woman whom I would marry told me that I must not feel guilty. It was inevitable, she said. Old loves. They do hang on.

Sunlight-yellow dust floats into my bedroom. I try to remember Athena. I try to focus upon Athena. What comes to me is the face of another girl—I see her hair, smell the childlike scent of her body, hear her laugh as she squeezes my hands—those boy's hands.

I am uneasy, and then I think that Mrs. Spacedon wouldn't have minded. Love, she often said, is love.

Marked

~~~~~~~~

I have always been good at making associations. As a result I receive terrific scores on personality tests. Take this list of traits labeled A, B, C, D, E, and F. Which one doesn't belong? I would select C for *bad*. Can you blame me—A is *icy* and B is *smooth*—already *bad* sticks out like a sore thumb.

Bad is an interesting word that can lead directly to *terrible*—as in tragedy—with portents like the cracked glass or the meaningful date. When I was living with Arno, our relationship didn't contain enough pain to be even bad. I didn't leave that man because he was dying of cancer or I found a lipstick in our bed or he confessed to homosexuality. I left him one day after we sat and talked—he had wants, I had yearnings. He said maybe we should try it apart. I had my back up, I said sure. Then we were separate. And it was strange, it was as if we had never been together.

The next thing I heard was that he had gone West. Later I got a postcard from the World's Almond Capital.

I recovered from this. People I knew came to New York. Imelda and her husband Marsh came to New York. It was January when she called me. Imelda got my telephone number from my Aunt Beulah in Wisconsin. "Come over," Imelda said to me. "We'd love to see you. Wait until you meet Marsh—you'll love him."

Imelda and I had gone to the same schools. I didn't remember that we were friends. I couldn't exactly recall her face. But it was January, it was snowing, it was Saturday morning. "Love to," I said. Anyway, they lived only four blocks away on First Avenue.

Exactly whom I was going to see, I didn't know. But waving from a second-floor window was this woman. That must be Imelda. I walked up the stairs, even though their building had an elevator. Imelda opened her door, grabbed my shoulders, kissed my cheek. "This is great," she said.

I kissed her back.

"Marsh went out to get bagels," she said. "But the coffee is ready."

They had a coatrack in a little hall. I pulled off my boots, they weren't dripping so I left them on a square of tile. The coat I hung up. Their apartment was nicer than mine. The rough-textured walls were white, setting off the furniture which was covered with decals of flowers or painted stripes or just bleached wood. There was a long pine chest in the living room, a couch draped with a red and white checked quilt. The wide windows were covered with white shades that had a random pattern of leaves, the skeletons of leaves. The place looked like something.

"Nice stuff," I said.

Imelda waved her hand at the room. "This," she said. "We shipped. All this is from when mother closed up the big apartment—this we had since I was a kid—when you used to come over."

I could have sworn I'd never seen anything in this room before.

Marsh came in. He too was new to me. He was from Philadelphia. He pumped my hand. "My goodness," he says. "I've heard a lot about you."

I stared at him, this man wearing a red and black checked lumberman jacket, a thick woolen cap, monster gloves. But best were the boots. The boots came halfway up his calves, thick laced boots. How long did it take him to lace them up? There was only a quarter inch of snow on the ground, there was an IRT stop across the street, and this man was dressed like the Lord of the Manor prepared to tramp across his land.

Imelda heated the bagels, set out the cream cheese, poured the coffee, and then we were seated across from each other.

"How have you been?" Imelda says. "I keep up with you, you know."

How? I write Aunt Beulah twice a year, messages inside cards.

"What do you think of our place?" Marsh said. "You should have seen these rooms before Imelda fixed them up—she's a genius. She stenciled the window shades herself."

"Great," I said. "Marvelous."

"Stenciling is fun—it's therapy. I've been in New York a month," Imelda said. "I haven't spoken to a single woman in one month—just the women in the doctor's waiting room."

"And suddenly here I am—serendipity," I said.

Marsh stared at me. He wasn't friendly.

*   *   *

I started seeing Imelda once, twice a week. We became daytime buddies. She would bring up events, dances, parties, a Sunday swim at the Lake. Not me, I'd tell her. Remember the Rooneys? she'd say. No, I'd say. Sure, she'd say. Well I didn't. Whom did I run with in those days? No one she'd know.

Most of the time Imelda walked to my apartment. "The streets are filthy," she complained. "I saw a man urinating right through the metal gate into the drugstore doorway."

"You're in the city to stay," I said to her. "Accept it."

Imelda rubbed her belly. "I hate being pregnant in New York," she said.

"You'll grow to love the city," I said.

"You're not pregnant," Imelda said. "Anyway I get lost, Cissie. Truly, I get lost. Marsh says look around—he says soon you'll find a sign that says this way to the George Washington Bridge. Follow it. I drove to Yonkers last week and went to Cross County. Our malls at home were better. People say the East Coast has it all."

We were walking down Broadway on the sunny side of the street. I was taking Imelda to the Strand Book Store. I was showing her the sights. At the corner the light turned red. "Ba-bay, baby, oh ba-bay, baby," crooned an old woman squatting by the curb, the outline of her thick pedestal thighs reassuring, else how could she keep that position. She moved a woven wicker baby carriage back and forth. In the carriage was a lump of dirty rags.

Imelda looked away, crossed herself.

"Why did you do that?" I asked.

"It'll mark me," Imelda said. "Mark the baby."

"You don't believe that? Come on, you don't believe that?"

Imelda pushed strands of hair from her face. "No," she said. "No, I don't. But why take chances." She patted her stomach.

"You can't do anything to a baby by *seeing* something," I said.

"Wait until it's you," Imelda said. "When you are the one going to have a baby—you'll see that different things matter. I mean if this baby were born peculiar for instance—I'd always blame myself. I would love to go home to have the baby, but Marsh said no. Marsh said New York was home. This is not home."

We went into the bookstore. "Look around," I said. "Buy."

We each purchased books. Imelda relaxed. I carried her bag and mine. Outside we bought ice cream from a cart.

"See," I said, "how nice the city can be."

I walked her home.

I type invoices in the evenings for a multinational. I work the four-thirty to midnight shift. How can you stand that? Imelda had asked. I said I didn't mind at all. The hours suit me, I said.

It was almost one a.m. I had just come home. The ringing was sharp but welcome. My voice when I answered was careful. I thought it was a man. There were several who might have called. But it was Imelda. "Cissie," she whispered, "I'm scared."

"What?"

"The landlady," Imelda said. "My landlady is putting a curse on the baby."

"Isn't she the woman who always sweeps? She's an ordinary woman, Imelda. Just a plain, old woman."

"She came out into the hall, Cissie. It was six o'clock, I was taking out my key. She kept winking at me. The water's bad, she said, and wiped her forehead with the edge of her apron. All her aprons are black—black flannel aprons."

"Imelda," I said, "she's got something wrong with her eyelids—she's always winking. Even *I* have seen her do that."

"No," Imelda said. "No."

I imagined her shaking her head for emphasis.

"Go back to sleep," I said. "It's the middle of the night."

"An omen," Imelda said. "The baby will be marked."

"No one is marking the baby," I said. "That's impossible."

"Wrong," Imelda said.

She hung up.

In the morning Imelda called back. "I'm sorry," she said. I had just awakened, I hadn't washed, I hadn't brushed my teeth. "I'm sorry I called you last night. Did I wake you? The problem was I got an unexpected telephone call earlier. I was so frightened. It was my oldest brother. He hasn't called me in three, four years. I thought right away someone had died."

"I understand," I said. "Everyone is entitled to a nightmare once in a while. Anyway, everything is all right. What does the doctor say? Everything is normal?"

"Yes," Imelda said. "He says it's all right. He says I'm watching my weight nicely."

"See," I said.

Imelda wanted me to come over for dinner on Sunday evening. I said no, another appointment. It wasn't a lie. I was going out with one of the night supervisors. Besides I knew that Marsh didn't like me. He said that I was a cold weather friend, he told that to Imelda. He said that all her friends from long ago—from when she lived on what he termed the prairies—were cold weather friends. Actually there wasn't a prairie to be seen. He had his states mixed up.

The telephone rang at four o'clock in the morning. It was not dawn. "I heard a screech this afternoon," Imelda said in a hoarse whisper. "A sound like a rooster being hurt."

"Feathers!" I said. "A rooster on First Avenue? Maybe the sound of a subway train stopping short, maybe kids fighting in the alley."

"A rooster," Imelda said, her voice beginning to shake, vowels rising. "Something was being done to it. The baby kicked at that moment—not really a kick, it was a scratch, a scratch within."

"No, it wasn't," I said.

"It was."

I thought I heard Marsh's voice in the background, the words indistinct. Imelda hung up.

After a moment I lifted the receiver off the hook and buried its buzzing beneath a cushion. I went to sleep.

Next time Imelda called it was three in the morning. Her voice as breathless as if she'd just stopped running.

"How come you have such courage," Imelda said. "You didn't marry. You didn't get married right away like I did—like Anne Marie did—like the rest of us."

"I'll get married," I said. "I will."

"If I have his baby, I am bound to Marsh forever and forever."

"Don't be foolish," I said. "Divorce is always possible. Everyone has divorce somewhere—children don't stop that."

"Maybe not—the divorce—but the binding is still there. And suppose I don't love him. Sometimes I awaken at night and I see Marsh beside me and I know I don't love him. It passes. But it happens. Then forever and forever, I must see his child."

"I don't think it's like that," I said.

"Did you know," Imelda said, "that there is a high incidence of fetal death in utero? That the cause of many degenerative diseases of the brain is unknown?"

Marsh worked in a building on Thirty-fourth and Fifth. The firm was listed in the telephone book. I called him at his office.

"Suppose she went home," I said to Marsh, "I mean just until the baby is born?"

"Home? When were you last back there?"

I hesitated. "Well," I said, "no one in my family lives there anymore."

"Imelda's mother," Marsh said, "has a two-room apartment in a special housing complex—and then later you can move into their nursing home. They call it Palm Gardens— snow most of the year, and they call it Palm Gardens. Her father is buried in Calvary. Imelda's younger brother is married and lives in Indianapolis, never mind the other one. What would she go back to? You make it sound like some ancestral home waiting for her. Maybe Imelda shouldn't see you for a while."

"All right with me," I said.

"The cab driver got lost," Imelda said. "All the cab drivers seem to get lost. Then just as we found a cop to ask, I saw a woman dancing on the street corner with one of those caps on the ground for coins. One leg—she was dancing on her left leg—balancing her body on the other side with a crutch—the stump was bandaged with bits of cloth, tape, safety pins. I felt the baby's movement—one leg kicking against the left side—just one."

I hung up quietly.

At four o'clock, the sun was low, I left my apartment to go to work. The early-evening crew jokes a lot. We can do this in our sleep we say. Production is up, though. I type all the invoices for the territory of New England. If the opportunity ever came up, I could win a contest for naming the largest number of cities in New England.

In Imelda's eighth month, I woke up one morning in my chilled bedroom. I woke up clear-eyed and sharp. He forced me, Imelda said. I didn't want this to happen, she said. I didn't want a child, I wasn't ready for a child. He forced me, I tell you. Another time she denied it. We talked about children, she said, it was our mutual decision.

Imelda and I sat at a table in a coffee shop on Lexington. Outside, staring through the window, was a woman, her grey hair cut in short spikes, a thousand tiny horns. I imagined some delousing procedure—the woman struggling, the scissors still moving. She wore tight black pants and a big grey tweed sweater. Her eyes glowed, polished crystals shining with madness, with fierce immediate thoughts without backing. She was shouting. "Blast him! Blast you! Blast him!"

A man from the coffee shop went out and chased her away.

Imelda sat with her back to the window. She saw nothing.

She fingered a large charm hanging from a thick black cord around her neck. I thought it was a carved stone. But when I reached over and touched it, the charm was ceramic with a small mold hole. A piece of commercial pottery.

"What is it?" I asked.

"A monkey," she said. "A monkey god. And later—the baby must always have a touch of red on his clothing to ward off evil spirits."

"I have met someone," I told Imelda. "I cannot be called at all hours."

"She's upset," Marsh said.

I'll say that for him, even now, asking for my help, you could hear in his voice that he didn't like me. He couldn't pretend to like me. "If she needs psychiatric care," he said. "I can't afford that."

"It's temporary," I said. "I'm certain that it's temporary."

"But suppose," he said, "suppose she does something to herself or to the baby."

"She won't," I said.

On Saturday I went to the library on Forty-second Street. I sat in the reading room all day like a schoolgirl. I read about babies. Primordial germ cells, microstomia, acrania, meromelia, cytotrophoblast, chorionic villus. The possibilities for something to go wrong dazed me. I thought of the daughter cells, the blastomeres.

I was making notes in a small spiral notebook. Then across the large room I saw someone. His name was Arno. I had lived with him once for three months. I was surprised that I could recognize him, that he looked the same.

He wore a navy blue pea jacket. He kept it on, even in that warm room. He turned the pages of a large, thick volume. Bound newspapers, I thought. He never looked up. Then a girl came and sat next to him. A blond girl wearing a green coat. He spoke to her and then they examined an item in his book. They were not strangers. He pulled back her chair and they left together. I cupped my face in my hands as they passed.

"It agarophobia," I told Imelda. "You suffer from agarophobia, a common ailment."

"What's that?" she asked.

"Only fear of pain," I said.

Marsh and Imelda moved to a larger apartment in Washington Heights, sunshine, more air. Imelda's baby was born at Lenox Hill Hospital. The doctor showed her the baby girl, she told me. A perfectly formed infant with smooth pink skin. I bought a white sweater set for the baby and took it to the hospital. Imelda looked wonderful. "A beautiful, beautiful baby," she said. "You can see her through the nursery window."

I stood outside the nursery and tapped on the window. A nurse moved a small wheeled bed closer. The baby slept, tightly swathed in a hospital blanket. Her hair was the color of wheat and a clot of red ribbon held a few strands.

Family Planning
in Summer

~~~~~~~~~

How did it happen that I never really wanted to be anything? A lack of proper heroines, one of my friends said. I read a lot of books, I read the complete Rafael Sabatini. All the time my mother read political theory. Is there a Veblen for kiddies? I read romances where the girl pulsed hungrily as the man leaned closer. And the wonder of it made me damp and itchy. I did a Wisconsin Centennial project and made collages of pioneer days, cutting off the technical parts of modern life so that the magazine pictures would fit. Considering the time, the era, some of my friends wanted to be nurses, some teachers, a few actresses. Me, I couldn't answer.

One thing I didn't want. I didn't want to be a mommy.

My mother was a good mother, a careful mother. She loved us. But I gave up games of house for other pursuits.

Running across fields of tall grass. What's there? I wondered. I decided to be an entomologist.

Baby, One

I knew a woman who had five babies, they stumbled
around her ankles. She was kind, good-natured, she steered
her body carefully past them. After a while, she willed
them to the community.

I am not motherly by nature, despite my admiration for
other women's babies. I smile at those children, I lavishly
praise their appearance, I send them presents. It's a question
of proper heroines. A lifetime spent in movies, with love.

There I am—blooming forth.
   You are pregnant, my dear.
   Was I ever pregnant before?
   Perhaps.
   I am pregnant now. I am deeply pregnant, cells prolif-
erating, the oogonia enlarging. Isn't that wonderful? The
oogonia.
   I am pregnant, I am married, and I am sixteen dollars into
next week's salary. An advance, sir. And Masterson, his
brown-toned teeth glistening in the fluorescent morning,
saying too many pretties, Cissie. Mustn't spend more
than we make.
   But passing out the dough, nevertheless.
   Mustn't upset Cissie. Cissie is a damn good typist. No
one can tap-tap her bitten fingernails like our Cissie.

I would have sworn that you could bet on pregnancy. A
sure thing, I would have said. But first the doctor said I

wasn't pregnant, then that same doctor said I was. "You'd think," I said to Raoul, "that after all these years, science would have such simple knowledge down pat."

"Yes," Raoul said and closed his book. The book was about the theory of diminishing returns. "It is definite then?"

"Right," I said, "this time the doctor spit over his left shoulder and said absolutely. I'm three months."

We nodded at each other. Things happen, the women at the office said. Would my mother have agreed? Not if you're careful, she would have said, not if you're careful.

In point of fact, (a) we weren't careful, and (b) we weren't loaded with money. We were what you would call small-time spenders. We were in Iowa City, we had an apartment on Market Street. We lived on my ten little fingers and Raoul's teaching assistantship.

"How long do you think they'll let you work?" Raoul asked.

"To the end," I said. How could I be replaced? My speed was incredible. The paper-attacker, Masterson said. No, they would not immediately get rid of me. Maybe move me to the back office.

"We'll apply for student housing," Raoul said.

There was, of course, nothing else to do.

We went straight into economies. We changed our habits, abandoned the evenings at the Airliner, forgot the monthly trips to Curt Yocum's to feast on rosy-pink beef. I hugged Raoul, and he hugged back. It'll be all right, we whispered.

These are the stages of pregnancy.

We went into dreaminess, we became nostalgic, and from there we went right into genetic damage.

"Exactly what did your brother Horace have?" Raoul asked.

I turned around, I was tearing lettuce leaves into a bowl, the bowl was rubbed with garlic. Horace was not a bad memory. He was a good memory. The sweet face, the nice kid. "Who knows? I never knew," I said. "He died a baby. Four is a baby."

The answer was not satisfactory.

Raoul tapped lightly on the top bar of the ladder-back chair. "You must have *known* something?"

"Nothing," I said. "Maybe my mother didn't pursue it." Was that true? I could see my mother staring at Horace. We all stared at Horace.

"When you are contemplating having a baby," Raoul said, "it is important to think of these things."

"We are not contemplating," I said sharply, "we are there. Anyway, think about my brother Sylvester—he's *ten* times smarter than you."

Was it over? With Raoul the wheedler—never. "Think," he said. "What were the expressions on Horace's face? How well did he walk? Try to recall any strange conversations about him."

So I waited for the right moment.

"And yours," I burst out triumphantly, it was Saturday. I savored the moment, enjoying the surprise. "You're big on my heredity. What about yours? What do we know about your family? What could you be hiding?" Never mind the cruelty, I wouldn't stop. "Didn't you tell me about an uncle with stubs for fingers? Machinery did it, you said—or was he born that way? They tell anything to kids. And hysteria? You told me enough about certain episodes—didn't you?"

I had him!

*   *   *

My fingers began to swell. I threaded my wedding ring onto a chain to wear around my neck. My ankles ached. Was the air conditioning strong in the back office? I fanned myself, making pleated papers from insurance forms, carrying forward carbon stains from paper to paper. The telephone rang often. It was an office, a place of work. Who? I yelled and slammed down the receiver. My obstetrician would see me only on Wednesday afternoons, it was a clinic, my time was not my own. How fast did I type? My fingers loitered over the keys.

I did it to myself, but I would not tell Raoul. It was in my sixth month. I had lost interest. Masterson touched my shoulders, damp fingers closing over bra straps. You'll make a crackerjack mother, he said. He stared at the papers on my desk, the miscellany of pens, the wire basket heavy.

They gave me a going-away shower. I said no, but they misunderstood. I was not being shy. There was home-baked angel food cake, a pile of yellow and green sunsuits, white sweaters. Someone folded the wrapping paper. You can use it again, he said.

How swiftly we moved, a whirl of boxes and we were done, planted in married student housing, one half of a Quonset hut. The moving was terrible. Raoul sweating there in summer shorts as he put together the metal frame for the bed, hoisted the mattress up, and then reestablished the bricks and boards for the bookcase. Got to study, he said. He was gone.

Summer is a bad time to be pregnant. You want to be beautiful in summer. The nights are long in summer, the air is damp and hot. You want to dance and be remarkable in summer.

My legs felt chafed, actually my thighs.

How shall I pass the time? My only friends were the women with whom I had worked and now we were separated. The heat made me unattractive. My hair flew into knots of curls.

"Do something," Raoul said. "Make baby clothes."

Oh the idiocy. Did we own a sewing machine? And me—hadn't he noticed that I could hardly thread a needle. "We'll buy," I said.

There were blotches on my belly where flesh stretched too much. I wore secondhand smocks.

The names of my neighbors are Sharon, Margaret Rose, Louise, Maribelle, Rosemary. All their children ride tricycles. The women don't smile at each other too much, living as we do side by side, it would be dangerous.

The woman I hate is named Arden. Her husband is also a graduate student in my husband's department. It would have been better if I liked her, our schedules were the same. "I don't understand," Raoul said. "She seems all right. They are even quiet and they live right here."

I hate Arden. I hate the inside of her house, as metal and small as mine. Arden has a pine rolltop desk, an easy chair covered with bluebird plaid wool, a spinet piano, an oval rug of brilliantly colored bits of red and yellow and blue. All from my family, Arden said, I inherited them. I hate Arden, her family, and perhaps even the small thin boy who silently pedals away at her side.

*   *   *

The Graduate Students' Wives Club invited me to a meeting. They served lemon meringue pie. I didn't like its runny softness. I tore up their next invitation—the RSVP card with its matching envelope. Let them guess!

I became a compulsive reader of the notices on bulletin boards, and bulletin boards were everywhere. Rides to Waterloo. Tutoring—endless tutoring. Math made simple. What was for sale? Unimaginable items. Bicycles readily described as worn and rusted. Share expenses to D.C. If I really liked a notice, I claimed it, taking also the thumbtack.

I read my findings to Raoul.

"You're keeping me awake," Raoul complained. "I can't study when I'm tired."

Did I care?

"Tired," I said. "Be tired! Does it matter to me what you want."

"What I want," Raoul said, "is to be done with your moods, finished with calming your ways, through with it all. I cannot be roused by you."

"Roused! Roused!" I shrieked.

Raoul turned on another light. His body, I noticed, was tanned.

"How can you face them?" he said.

"Who?" I yelled.

"All the people out there listening to you—hearing you."

"Tin can house," I said.

I took up walking. I walk down streets and look in windows. The houses of permanent people. Pregnant women come out of many of those houses. The women smile at me, they nod. Do we have a secret handshake, a code?

How long can you walk? A little. Mostly in the morning, because by afternoon the heat descends and chews up the shade and the slightest edge of coolness. I go to the city pool. I sit by the side of the pool, my feet touching the water. I stay dry, making only the shortest of waves.

The university library is cool. I ease myself onto a wooden chair. There are plenty of books about pregnancy. Elephants carry for thirty-six months, their post-partum must be full of woe. I leave the animal kingdom and go into teratology. The illustrations are of miniature Lon Chaneys.

Pregnancy through the ages, pregnancy through the neighborhood. It's all right if you're married. If not—oh boy—*trouble.* "Have you ever thought about that?" I asked Raoul. "I mean, what a phrase—*in trouble.*" I drained a pot of spaghetti, the steam was a small geyser. "Think about it," I said. "Trouble-trouble and everyone knows what that means, don't they? No one thinks the girl got caught with her hand in the till or shoplifting at the A & P. No siree—that girl has been with a man. That girl is in carnal trouble."

Raoul looks up at me. "I'm studying for a test," he says.

Pregnant women—was J. of Arc ever pregnant? Could you fit into a suit of armor with your big belly? As a matter of fact, do bellies recognize each other? The little babes sending out a silent hello to the other little babes in the bellies of passing women?

"What do you have on?"
Me? What would I have on?
"On your feet," he says.

"My shoes."

"And my socks," Raoul said. "My brown socks."

"They're comfortable."

"They look terrible—they look incredibly awful—because your slacks are too short."

"Sez you!"

When I was fourteen I had a crush on a pregnant girl. An obsession for her. What had I wanted? Secrets. I was in search of secrets. The Mysteries of Life! Oh wow—peeking into books, at pictures of the growing fetus. The bun in the oven.

Did I suspect that Raoul had someone? Someone named Jean whose lipstick was orange and whose hair was red-smoke. Can you follow him everywhere? Can you lumber across the hills wearing those sturdy, correct shoes? Do his neat fingers make nice to some girl?—a graduate student—better yet a younger one still prone to dyed-to-match sweaters. Does he tell her about his parents lopped off too soon, about the swell aunt and uncle who raised him, the uncle a Methodist minister?

Jean sends a birthday card, it says *Have A Happy Day!* How did I get my hands on it? I say I found it on the floor. I searched his books, his folders, his notes. Dropped indeed. Imagine him believing that. A fellow student, he says. And did you remember?

I pat my stomach, on whom I blame everything.

I can see now that while I am in the hospital in my narrow ward bed, he will couple with Jean, bring her to our house, no fear of discovery. Drunk with new fatherhood, he'll seal her birthday greetings with a kiss. They'll laugh and whisper. Before dawn, he'll take her away. I'll lie in my bed. I'll be one person by then.

I am two people.
Whom shall we name the baby after?
We shall name the baby after the dead. Are they pleased to hear the song of their name again?

My partner, the obstetrician, says any day now.
A pat on the shoulder.
Raoul moved to the couch.
I understood—I am the restless body, I am the kicking spirit, I am the stretching soul.

I sat at my table, sipping my tea, leaning back in my chair, my favorite position, with the chair balanced on the two back legs, leaning dangerously against the wall. Her name was Barbara, the child I had stalked, the little pregnant girl I had loved. And she had told me nothing, not a word.

I bought two fans. I turned them on. They just suck the hot air in, Raoul warned. Never mind, it was the noise I wanted, the blurring sounds. I needed time to contemplate, to prepare, to become an adept. I called to the dark creature in me. Wait, I said. But it moved on, away from me.

Baby, Two

The August Raoul was finishing his dissertation, my mother died. I was Vice President of the Graduate Students' Wives Club. I was pregnant, and we were sure this one would be a boy.
How did I know my mother had died? There were no

premonitions, it was not a day for deaths, being too bright and too early for shadows. Although there are certain signs—but what foretells?—is it the sudden breaking of a glass or the dropping of a particular utensil? The knife, for instance.

The telephone call came at ten in the morning from my cousin Bonnie. An accident, Bonnie said. Afterwards what I wanted to know was how Bonnie had found me. I had seen her once, twice—not even my mother's kin—a child of my father's side. An accident, Bonnie said. What? I kept saying. Repeat, please? It was hard to hear, to hush the baby Eleanor pulling at the hem of my skirt, a winding serpent around my leg. We were going shopping. We were always going shopping. I had promised Eleanor a bribe of cookies. What? I said into the telephone.

And all the time Eleanor shrieked, "Go! Go!"

"Yes," I said into the telephone. "Yes, I hear now."

I hung up.

Eleanor stared at me, her cheeks were flushed.

"I have a headache," I said. "Mommy has a headache."

"Go," Eleanor said, her plump legs firmly placed.

There were friends. Friends are the rock. I took Eleanor's hand. She struggled, suspecting the wrongness of the moment. Were we going shopping? "Purse," she shouted. Where was my purse?

I pulled her along. I went next door. "Sharon," I said, and knocked on the door.

The door opened. "What's wrong?" Sharon said staring at me. "You sick?"

Eleanor pulled free. She saw Sharon's little boy. Robert was watching *Romper Room*. He had a glass of milk, a package of Oreos.

"There's been an accident," I said. "My mother is dead."

*　　　　*　　　　*

Friends are everything. Sharon made me sit down on her couch. She washed my face with a wet washcloth. It was she who called Margaret Rose. Margaret Rose was organized, didn't she have three children. She was called in times of birth and death.

Margaret Rose got through to Raoul's departmental office. I could hear her arguing, they didn't call graduate students to the telephone, they didn't look for them either. But Margaret Rose wouldn't be stopped. Then Raoul came home.

There were people around. The doctor was soothing. It's all right, he said to my husband. She can make the trip.

Friends brought food to the apartment, as if it were a wake here without the dead. Cakes and pies and fruit. I saw Eleanor, her hands clutching crumbs of food, her lips jelly-blue. I feared for her, I had a premonition as I saw the glow of her eyes. Fat Eleanor, I thought. Poor fat Eleanor.

Raoul didn't want me to go to St. Louis alone, but there was the cost of another ticket, and then Eleanor became hysterical and screamed, "Daddy! Daddy!"

"I'll be all right," I said. I promised to call. I never told Raoul that no one met me at the airport. Bonnie's responsibility to me dimmed by separations, divorces, inheritances.

How did she die?" my brother Sylvester asked.

"An accident," I said. "A car, an automobile."

"I'll fly in tonight," he said.

And before he arrived, I knew the tale.

It was the sort that makes small paragraphs in the back pages of newspapers and does not happen to anyone you know. She was riding with two friends, it was four o'clock in the afternoon, when for reasons unknown, the women decided to race a train to a crossing. Three middle-aged women after an afternoon shopping at the Southside Mall, filled with weak drinks, giggling with joy and loneliness, accelerator down.

The man my mother had lived with was named George. They were together for nine years. When my mother died, she was living alone in her apartment. George was not there. He has Parkinson's, my mother wrote, he trembles and cannot bear life or touch. She would have tended him, he could have stayed with her. But quite suddenly he fears that. It's better, he says, and goes to Sacramento to stay with his son, a son past forty and burdened with wife and memories. The son will care for him. George is older than my mother, he is now eighty. But he outlives her. That kind outlives us all. He sent a wreath to the funeral. It says *Sweetheart* in gold letters on red ribbon. First, I would have the funeral director remove it, destroy it, but then I think, who am I to do that. Not my decision, I let the wreath stay. My father sends a blanket of white roses. They say nothing.

Besides my brother and me, my mother has one living relative close enough to call. It is her sister Beulah, who lives in a residence for the retired. She is much older than my mother, she is the age of George. I was right about who outlives whom. I telephone her. "Mother died," I say.

"I'll not come," she says. "She insulted me."

"What?"

"She says to me fry in hell. Her last words to me."

I hang up. I believe that she will be sorry, I anticipate the evening when Aunt Beulah calls, her heart bitter and filled with salt. Dead, she'll shriek, oh not dead, never dead. Let me speak to her, let me see her. She'll cover her head with the skirt of her apron and pull at her hair and wear a piece of black ribbon with a ceremonial tear. All of this, of course, will come too late.

Sylvester was never my favorite brother. Never mind that Horace died at age four. "As soon as my wife gets her degree," Sylvester said, "we're off to California."

He sat across from me. We were not at ease.

"Can I leave you with all this?" he said.

He meant the apartment.

"Yes." I nodded. "Is there anything you want from here—from mother's things?"

Sylvester flushed. "No," he said, "no, honest."

"All right," I said. "I'll either sell this or give it all away. I don't know."

"You do whatever seems best," Sylvester said.

"I'll send you your share, if I sell," I said.

"No," he said, "you're doing all the work. I don't want anything."

"All right," I said.

I called Raoul in Iowa City. "I have to close up the apartment," I said.

"How long?" he asked.

I could hear Eleanor crying in the background. "Mommy! Mommy!" she yelled.

"A week," I said. "It'll take me a week."

"That long?"

"I'll hurry," I said.

*　　　*　　　*

I turned on the air conditioning in the apartment. The building had central air conditioning. The knob had a setting labeled *Cold,* and the three rooms quickly chilled. It felt wonderful. I thought the air soothed the baby within me. You wouldn't guess the month was August. I pulled the drapes against the brilliance of the heat. I used my mother's shampoo, brushed my teeth with her toothpaste. At night I slept on sheets as cold and smooth as ice.

"Your mother was a fine woman," said Mr. Soyle, the building superintendent. "Would it be possible to show the apartment—I won't, if you mind. But your mother kept a spic-and-span place—it makes a good impression when an apartment is furnished and clean."

"All right," I said.

I hung up my clothes, picked up the newspapers, put the dishes into the dishwasher.

In a dresser drawer I found the album. Many of the photographs were gone, some that I remembered from childhood. Pictures of my mother and father on vacations, backgrounds unknown, arm in arm and smiling. They were gone. Also the small sepia-tinted one from their wedding day, my mother with a garland of flowers woven through the coils of her hair. I would have kept that picture, but it was not to be found. My mother had plowed her way through them all. There were pictures of me and of Sylvester. I put his into an envelope to send to him. Those of Horace I kept. In the photographs he looked less happy than I remembered. I thought he had smiled most of the time.

The man's name was Linga. He had just moved to the city from Minneapolis. "I'm going into my brother's business," he said. "I sold hardware on Hennepin Avenue for thirty years—and finally threw in the wrench." He winked at me. "My brother owns a restaurant," he said. "Northern Italian. Here." He gave me a card. "You stop by before you leave town, bring anyone. The first meal is free."

I smiled back.

Mrs. Linga did not speak. She's a mute, her husband explained.

"What I see," he said, "I like. I mean everything. We sold our place, colonial furniture, solid maple. I shipped nothing, zero, zilch. Mr. Soyle says you're planning to dispose of this stuff. I'll buy it—everything—kit and caboodle."

I stared at him. "All right," I said.

He hesitated. "Is it too hard for you—I mean if we took also the dishes, pots, linen?"

"No," I said.

He didn't bargain. The price was good. I shook his hand. He poked his wife, she held out her hand.

Basically, I didn't think she was shy.

I put clean sheets on the bed, waited until they had absorbed the icy chill of the room. We slept there, the baby and I, for seven days. I wondered if I had imprinted the baby with this memory of cold, sweet possession of self.

The Survivors
of Mrs. Spacedon

~~~~~~~~~

Dear Sylvester,

I hope you receive this letter. It was only last Saturday when I decided to write to you, just seven days ago. In sight, in memory, I guess. Last Saturday we were doing the same thing, you and I. Patrons of that new mall just north of Beyfield. I thought for a moment that I was deceived—seeing visions—that the man was not you. But then, of course, I knew that was you by Frank's Sportswear turning quickly to the right then through the drug display of Top-Mart, cutting the corner into Fast Chicken then a left past the little indoor fountain near the spray of plastic tulips. I lost you. It was you. I should have called your name, I regret that I didn't, but I was certain that I would overtake you, surprise you with my greeting. But no, you were gone. Either on the escalator to the next level or into some opening I had not seen. I lingered for a while in the center courtyard, but you did not reappear.

I checked the telephone book, but your family name wasn't listed. You must have been visiting someone. I would have been defeated, but I remembered that aunt of yours, the many times I dropped you off at her house. No luck—she too was not in the book. So I drove the neighborhood. I must have been destined to find you, Sylvester. Old Madeleine Miller, still alive, standing by the curb, broom in hand. Try Palm Court, she said. His Aunt Beulah is in the Palm Court Home for the Retired.

Bingo!

As an example of how thoroughly I wanted to reach you, Sylvester, I went to Palm Court with a box of chocolates. Your Aunt Beulah looks fine. All dressed up she came into the Day Room. Yes, she said, I remember you. Are they soft ones? she said. As a matter of fact, I assured her there wasn't a caramel in the box. Is Sylvester in town? I asked. And that, my boy, was a mistake. You expect me to know! she shouted. You think he comes to see me! Well, five minutes later—the one fact I didn't doubt was that she was certainly not senile.

I got the address—an address. Although she was reluctant to confess—it appears that you remember her enough to send two checks a year. She tore off a corner from an envelope. He's either here or he isn't.

Those are the terms, Sylvester. You are either here or you aren't.

Sylvester, I haven't seen you since you and my sister Athena parted. I know a lot of people thought it was the breakup of Romeo and Juliet. But it wasn't—and it turned out all right, didn't it? I mean my sister is married and living in Baltimore and happy as far as anyone knows. Beulah said you married too—and children.

In many ways, Sylvester, I always considered you a friend—a true family friend—I always ignored the fact that you were hardly more than a boy when I first met you. And I personally always wished you had come back to see us. I forgave you. I'm sure in time Mama would have forgiven you too.

Mama is dead, Sylvester. Mrs. Spacedon was, as you know, an energetic person, and the end was swift. She rests in Calvary on Raillor Road. Even the funeral was what we believed she would have wanted. Donna picked out the dress—one of those Bemberg sheer ones Mama loved, endless rows of flowers blooming in tropical colors. Daggert of Daggert Brothers was not pleased, but they laid her out in the Madison Room dressed as we wanted and buried beneath brilliant vertical rows of floribunda. Our dear mother, *our* Mrs. Spacedon.

You should see the family house. You would not recognize the house, Sylvester. It is painted now. The house has been completely changed. We who are the survivors cherish, collect, and place different objects. There are no bits of crochet lying about, no batik table runner that Mama dyed in the water from onions. Where is the picture of FDR's Fala? The snow-capped mountain carefully clipped from a calendar of another year? The very knob of the newel post is different. We knew that Mrs. Spacedon would not mind. The vapors that are now Mama roam elsewhere. She loved to move about.

If only I had called out your name. Because last week William was here. Yes, our William was actually here in town. He telephoned us from Dayton. I'll have only one day, he says, but how could I come across country without stopping.

What could I do? Come at once, I said. We'll give you your old room. The floor is now burnished pine. The walls are cool white. There are the silver leaves of lantana on the windowsill.

Can't put you out, William says. A motel. That way Kyle and I won't be a bother to anyone. Anyway, I'll want to get an early start when we hit the road again.

What could I say? He is my only brother. So when William calls next, he has checked into the Holiday Inn under the bypass. Dinner, I say. Come right over and eat. Dropping in my tracks, William says. We came across country like Flash Gordon. We'll be over tomorrow.

There I was, Sylvester, feeling like I did when I spotted you near Top-Mart—filled with anticipation, and perhaps enjoying the anticipation. William is coming. Donna is just staring at me. Who needs to see him? she says.

Do you remember the photographs that used to be on the fireplace mantel? You chopped plenty of wood for that fireplace, didn't you, Sylvester? That's how we first met— you chopping wood for us. The photographs are gone. There are no photographs on the mantel, which Donna has sanded and scraped and chemically returned to bleached oak. She said she didn't know where the photographs were.

Did I give up? I remembered the top drawer of the buffet. There I found those photographs piled in a jumble of years and occasions. Mama was a great one for pictures. What did I find? I found one of Mama in a summer dress standing very straight in front of the azalea bushes, which were only half their present size then. Athena sitting on the front steps with some stray collie. William, pretending to fight, holding up his fists, clowning. Then the picture of me—the one that was always to the far left on the old mantel. I had my arm around Buddy Palmer's shoulders, his family moved to Toledo. It was my best picture, Mama said, so there it was on display.

I never forgot the day Donna arrived. I took her right over to the mantel. I was a kid all dressed up in my corduroy school pants and a white shirt to greet Donna. Donna was not like Athena at all. Athena had always been so reluctant. We'll have your picture up here, I told Donna. You know Donna. She was the same when she was a young girl—cheeky. Mean-spirited, she called it. But she wasn't. Donna pointed at Athena's picture. She the other girl? she asked. Yes, I said. Be your sister. Not my sister, Donna said. None of you are real relatives.

I could hardly sleep, Sylvester. I was waiting for William.

And then there he was.

I took him for a walk around the neighborhood, which you wouldn't recognize either. Look, William says. What a change! He is astonished by the cathedral. It takes up an entire block. The Convent of St. Agnes is gone and the schoolyard and the two empty lots. The cathedral is old to me. It was built ten years ago. I didn't remember there were so many Catholics in the neighborhood, William says. Sure, I tell him, just across the street was that girl Rosemary whose sister was a nun. Then the family next to Lloyd and the one in the house with the fieldstone front. And Clarisse's family. How is Clarisse? William asks. Don't know, I said.

William's wife Kyle doesn't care about the neighborhood. No reason why she should. It's not her neighborhood. She plumped herself down in the kitchen with

Donna. That's where we found her when we came in for lunch. Donna laid plates of sliced cold tongue. There was a small pot of that fiery mustard you always used to like. A salad of lettuce and toasted croutons, and the wooden bowl rubbed with garlic. Donna takes after Mama. She puts out a good table.

William gets right down to the nitty-gritty. Tell me, he says, you two run into any trouble when you married each other? Now I knew this was coming, Sylvester. Maybe even *you* would have asked—although with some hesitation. The question doesn't bother me. Neighbors, friends, and now William. You know we're not blood kin, I said. Not cousins or anything. None of us. I know that, William said, biting into the tongue. Still we always called Donna our sister. The Spacedon kids, isn't that what we said?

True, I said, but there wasn't any legal adoption for her. I mean that's the difference.

What I did, Sylvester, when Donna came to be our sister, was to take her to school. She's been living with our father, I lied, but now she's back. Everyone accepted that. Mama had little faith in legalities. Mama was always afraid that someone would come and claim us.

Donna never talked about her natural mother—at least not until we were married. It's none of your business, she used to say. Her mother came from Chicago. Donna thought that there were some letters from Mrs. Spacedon. She thought maybe her mother and Mrs. Spacedon had been friends. Anyway, she was brought to us. For the longest time, Donna confessed, I thought Mama got money for keeping me. Then I found out it wasn't so—she became Mama, and I forgot the rest.

*   *   *

What would have pleased Donna was a few comments about the house. I kept waiting for William to say something. I mean Donna did it all. Hard work, she always said, but worth it. The house was built in 1855, she had verified the date. Even if it was a house in town, it was a fine one. The reconstruction inside and out took her six years. She recovered the chairs in authentic patterns from the period. William stood near the oriel staring through wavy glass. Some of the windows still have the original glass. It's none of my business, William says, but it must have taken guts to marry each other and stay around here.

Where were you, Sylvester, when William got married? Did we know you yet? Sure, we did. It was after William came home from the army. Athena was still in D.C. I tell you, seeing William once again at our table—I could feel the heat of the day he got married, the uncomfortable jacket I wore, the pleasure on Mama's face.

Mama sprang it on us. Pack your suitcases, she said. We are going to Duluth. Could we miss William's marriage? William was marrying in the month of June, doing it just right. Mama had a blue taffeta dress. Kyle's family had rented a hall for the reception.

We went there, Sylvester. A real orchestra playing. Neither Donna nor I had ever been to a wedding before. Mama's face flushed. She loves weddings, she says. The bride in white. The air full of honeysuckle. Mama danced the Mother's Dance with William.

Donna and me—we were watchers. We watched Kyle. She was blond and wore her hair in a row of short curls. She was a grown-up woman with that firmness that some women have. Donna stood leaning against a wall, she never moved. Donna had long brown hair that fell straight to her shoulders, and an unsoftened body. I thought that day that she was very beautiful, although for the moment Kyle was better-looking.

Mama never gives up. Back and forth she goes. Come to the buffet? she asks Donna. Shall I make you a plate? No Mama, Donna says. I'm all right, Mama. Clement will dance with you, Mama says, and motions to me. Come, Clement. Not on your life, says Donna.

Who tied the knot? William asks. I tell him. It was in October. Donna and I were married by Reverend Maas, who was willing. They only need one side of the church for his and hers, someone says. We heard that. For the party held in the house there was champagne and orange cake made by Aunt Margaret Laszcio who is not really an aunt but a second cousin of Mama's.

Actually, between William and Mama was a true legal bond. He was her ward. His mother left him four thousand dollars when she died. She lived in one of those back alley houses on Tenell Place. A born cleaner, she scrubbed all the time. Mama never believed in that. When William's mother got sick, Mama made her a special tisane.

Only right, William's father argued, to name him the boy's guardian. He wanted to take William out West. God's country, he said. Four thousand dollars, Mama said. William told the judge no dice, he'd stay here, same neighborhood, he said. He'd take Mrs. Spacedon.

At four o'clock I took William out to Mama's grave. First we stopped at a florist, William bought a spray of white lilies. She liked white, he says. He imagines that. I figured he'd looked at Donna's garden—she has white everywhere, white roses, white begonias, white portulaca. I always regretted not coming back for the funeral, William says. I understand, I say. Anyway, he says, I sent a wreath.

Afterwards we go back to the house for some drinks. Why did you stay around here? William asks. I mean, wouldn't it have been easier to go somewhere else?

That's what I once asked Donna. It's our house, she said. Mama was happy here. But it was true that some people made it hard. People being people. Even Dr. Wrinkler sitting at our table before our marriage and not asked to volunteer his opinion said—It's incest, kids. Any way you want to cut it—it's a form of psychological incest. Bull! Donna said. But she didn't sleep that night.

Listen, Sylvester, there was a time when I thought Donna liked William better. He was a handsome kid—better-looking than me. Then too, he was a soldier boy. Mama hung a star in the window. Donna knitted a muffler. We had a special Thanksgiving dinner in August for him. He came home on leave. Once I knocked on Donna's door and when I went into the room, William and Donna were sitting on opposite ends of the bed. I thought they had secrets. What's doing? I asked.

The day ends, and soon Kyle presents Donna with a package wrapped in gold striped paper. A lagniappe, she says. Inside there was a small bowl carved from chestnut wood. Donna smiled and kissed Kyle's cheek. Give my love to your children, she said. Kyle nodded. Our daughter lives in Buffalo, she said. We're sidetracking up there. The older boy stayed on the Coast. Things are tough for him.

Tough all over, William said. Before I lost my distributorship and the money went with the wind, we had the biggest damn pool you ever saw. And a live-in couple. Kyle didn't have to stir a rib. Then I said to her, Hell, I'll try the other coast. Lebensraum, that's what I need.

I found a camera, Sylvester, before William and Kyle left. If this turns out to be your address, I'll send you prints of the best pictures. We took turns holding the camera. Shots of all of us. The Spacedon clan. Then off they go—William and Kyle—waving down the road.

You're a married man, Sylvester. You know that we don't get away that easily. Donna had the look of gloom all over her face. What I am thinking is—I stuck her with Kyle for the whole day. Kyle? she says, as if I am nuts or something. Who cares about Kyle? I didn't mind her. It's you, she says. Taking William around like that. William, come see this. William, what do you think of that. After all these years—welcoming the little lamb.

In truth, Sylvester, what would she have had me do— bolt the door on my own brother? He's one of us, I said. Didn't Mama say that William became family the day he moved into the house. I reached for her, but Donna was quick. William, she said, didn't deserve Mama. To that I have the answer. She called him son, I say.

Son! Donna hoots. Some son that one! Take the time he came home discharged from the army. Remember the party Mama gave him, remember how she took him out and bought him all those new clothes because nothing fit him anymore. Then when he was off to Duluth to be with Kyle's family she gave him two hundred dollars—she almost cleaned out her bank account.

That's Mama, I say. Donna is holding up her hand—it means silence. Can you ever interrupt a wife, Sylvester?

I thought William was being sneaky. Something didn't smell right, Donna says. He had that big duffle bag with his army things. He wouldn't unpack. He wouldn't even open it. I knew that he was planning to haul the thing up to Kyle's. So I wait. And one day he's out, and I went up to his room to see what he had in that bag. The rat had plenty—gifts—the thing was full of stuff. Perfume. Trinkets. Bolts of cloth. The bastard! What did he give to Mama? Nothing, Clement. Nothing for Mama.

Donna starts crying. You can do nothing with Donna when she's crying. I went out onto the porch until she calmed down. In the late afternoon the shadow of the cathedral almost reaches our house. I think I am the keeper of all family memories. I think sometimes that Mama elected me to do that. So I have this scene from the day William came home still wearing his uniform. From Paris, William is saying to Mama. For you. He breaks the seal on the bottle. The seal means it's the real McCoy, he says. Mama giggles. She has never been given real perfume. William gives her a silver charm bracelet with a miniature Eiffel Tower dangling from it. The blue velvet is for a dress and the grey wool for a winter coat. Then William winks at Donna in secret conspiracy over Mama's pleasure. All the time, I'm leaning against the door and waiting my turn. Mama sees me and beckons and we are all in the circle of her arms.

It could have been that way, Sylvester. And you could have married my sister Athena. Mama would have called you son too. You and I would have been brothers. And that's how I think of you, Sylvester. I really do.

Love,

Your Brother
Clement Spacedon

Penny and Willie

~~~~~~~~~~

It came to Sylvester one day that his daughter Penny was always home before him when it rained. The realization surprised him. Was he particularly obtuse? He had been to the dentist that afternoon. Perhaps that was it—novocaine made him jumpy. Maybe it sharpened him too.

He was on the bus, the rain beating on the roof, the air warm and damp. At one stop schoolgirls flooded the bus with color, waves of little girls giggling, wearing Day-Glo–colored slickers and backpacks. They were eleven years old. He had a talent, an ability to assess the ages of little girls. He did this by comparing them to Penny. He suspected that this ability would atrophy in time. The girls moved to the back of the bus, shaking the water from their surrealistic backs. Pink, yellow-green, pure red.

Perhaps the sight of the girls triggered something. Some background thought he must have pushed away. The unimportant supplanting the important. He considered that. Wasn't that what he'd heard people did who were faced with terrible problems? This was not like that. This was just life. But still he had seen nothing. He was surprised. Because he loved his daughter. Therefore, why hadn't he noticed that Penny was always home before him when it rained. Penny regularly went to the library after school. Sylvester would be home for at least a half hour before she showed up—unless it was raining. The library wasn't on a bus line. She would have had to walk five blocks coming and going in the rain. Being home alone must have been preferable to that.

If he was right, then she would be waiting for him today. He could hear music coming from the apartment. He rang the bell instead of using his key. The music was loud, and Penny might not hear the door open, and he didn't want to startle her. He waited to see if she would use the peephole. That always worried him, but Penny looked through the hole and then opened the door. "Hi Daddy," she said. A book was draped across her arm— *Life in Ancient Rome.*

"Lower the music, please," Sylvester said. Penny made a face and crossed the room to the phonograph. She had her shoes off and Sylvester could see the blackened pads of her white socks. Her mother would look at them with distress. Joyce disliked dirty clothes. "Pigeon," Sylvester said. "How you doing, pigeon?"

"I turned on the oven already," Penny said, "like the note said. Start oven. Four hundred degrees. Turn on at five o'clock." She pushed back her long, dark hair.

My child, Sylvester thought, is such a thin pale girl. He would have to think through the significance of having realized Penny's unvarying schedule. He went to change his clothes before making the salad.

He always made the salad when Joyce printed *Salad* on the daily kitchen clipboard sheet. She never asked him to, but he did anyway. They ate out twice a week, more often if Joyce called up and said, "I'm bombed, dead, swept away." Then Sylvester would turn off the oven, and if a salad had been cut, he would empty the bowl into a plastic bag for the next day.

He started the salad, ripping up leaves of romaine and bits of chicory. Sylvester liked to put different ingredients in the salad, he experimented. Sometimes unsuccessfully, like the time he combined anchovies with bits of dried fig and scattered them among the greens; and once he had poured on red pepper flakes. No one had been able to eat those salads.

He sliced onions. Stupid, he had been stupid—worse than that. He had been unobservant of what was important. When had it rained last? A week ago—on Tuesday or maybe Wednesday. Penny had been home that afternoon too. Was that indicative of her life? When had the telephone rung for *her*—nor did Penny seem to go out regularly with friends on weekends. What about birthday parties? He was startled at the ache that arose, disturbing what he suspected must be his growing ulcer. He burned and at the same time felt the sensation of descending too quickly in an elevator. He poured a glass of milk and drank it slowly.

Sylvester designed jewelry. He had his own small office, was his own boss. He designed inexpensive, commercial-type jewelry. Once in a while he did something better—a single piece. A gift for someone, a client's wife or the client's girl friend. An artist, they would say, staring at a pin or earrings or a ring. A piece carefully crafted of excellent materials. That, Sylvester realized, was because they did not know any better. He was good—but that was it. He made gifts for Joyce and Penny too. Both had rings and necklaces and bracelets meticulously executed.

He had taken particular pleasure in the intricate enamel design on Penny's locket, which she wore all the time. Vines and blue morning glories spelled her name, if you stared long enough at the pattern.

Sylvester always left his office at four to miss the heaviest evening rush. He was home first—unless it rained. Joyce didn't arrive home until after six. He knew that he would speak to Joyce about Penny being alone. But he mustn't mention it to Penny. Did she mind? Of course she must. Was she unpopular? He winced. He envisioned her living a life alone. The music from the living room continued.

He waited after Joyce came home, waited until she had settled down, told the day's anecdotes. They were together in the kitchen. She was adjusting the salad dressing. "Listen," he said softly, "I think Penny is alone too much. Lonely."

Joyce licked the traces of oil from her finger. "Lonely?" she said. "Why do you say that?"

"When it rains," Sylvester said. "She's always home. Like she has no other girls to spend her time with."

Joyce looked at him. "What do you want her to do? Stand outside in the rain?"

Sylvester shook his head. "I'm not joking. I want her to be with other kids."

"Maybe," Joyce said, "she prefers to be alone. Just before you hit the teens, it's funny sometimes. Many girls prefer to be alone. Penny is quiet, shy, maybe a touch bookish."

"Don't analyze her that way," Sylvester said.

"I'm not." Joyce became defensive. "But she seems fine to me. Good grades, good spirits."

Sylvester said no more, feeling moderately intimidated. Joyce, after all, had been an eleven-year-old girl. Joyce also was a clinical psychologist. However, he noticed at dinner that Joyce observed Penny more closely, asking questions about what she had done that day.

Sylvester's parents had both worked, but one or another always seemed to be around when he came home. Then too he had a sister. He had seldom come home to an empty house. When Penny was younger, they had paid a woman to pick her up from school and take her to a special play group. She was too old for that now. He suspected that she would be horrified at any suggestion that she couldn't take care of herself.

The decision to get a dog was impossible. It was impractical. Therefore, he didn't mention it to Joyce. Not that she disliked dogs. No, she always stopped to watch the antics of puppies in pet store windows. But he knew that if he spoke of it, they would discuss the matter and sanely resolve that it was wrong. He would have added to the discussion his own valid reasons why it was impossible.

He began to read the advertisements in newspapers of pets for sale. What he wanted, he realized, was a puppy, but not too young—one past infancy, one trained or almost trained, one not too big. Sylvester himself had never had a dog. Early each morning he began to call likely prospects in Manhattan. It was not easy. He thought he could discern who really wanted to unload an animal, the eagerness, the hard sell, the emphasis on pedigree. It was different with Willie. "I'm getting married," the owner said, "and she, the lady I'm going to marry, has two dogs already. Two old poodles, one is five years old, the other eight. She can't give them up. Willie is young, only six months."

Sylvester made an appointment and went up to the young man's apartment. That was a good sign, he felt, an apartment-raised dog. Willie was a bull terrier, a small white dog with random black spots, spunky, with a mock ferocious manner that ended with his thoroughly licking Sylvester's hand. "He's yours," the man said, "if you can give him a good home. He's a wonderful dog."

Sylvester squatted and petted Willie, and the dog bounced and danced beneath his touch. "I'll take him," Sylvester said. The man nodded, his hands jammed into his pockets. His reluctance reassured Sylvester, the man did not want to part with the animal. "Seventy-five dollars was the advertised price," Sylvester said. He didn't even bargain.

"Yes," the man said. He went to his desk. "Here," he said. "Papers. Willie has papers. I'll get his stuff." The man hooked a slightly nibbled black leash onto the dog's collar, and he gave Sylvester a large grocery bag with an open package of dry dog food inside, a ball with stripes, and a large orange plastic bowl coated around the rim with a crust of dried dog food. Sylvester and the man shook hands. "So long, Willie," the man said.

Willie saw the leash. He trembled in anticipation of a walk. Once on the sidewalk, Sylvester suddenly felt self-conscious. He was a man with a dog. The puppy strained the length of the leash. "No," Sylvester said and tugged back. "This way," he said, and Willie followed. Sylvester waited until he was a block away and then tossed the paper bag into a wire trash basket. It was foolish, he knew, throwing away the food and everything. But he planned to get everything fresh. Everything new for Penny.

A red collar and leash, he decided. Would a taxi accept him and the dog? The driver didn't seem to care.

"A damn fool idea," Joyce whispered that evening. "What about our lease?"

"There are a dozen dogs in the building," Sylvester whispered back.

Penny was ecstatic, she was down on her knees as the dog enthusiastically leaped at her. "Mine?" she said. "Honestly, it's mine?"

"You bet," Sylvester said.

"Disease," Joyce said. "Does he have diseases?"

"No," Sylvester said. "Look at him—a perfectly healthy puppy."

"Has he got a name?" Penny asked.

The dog, pleased to be the center of attention, wiggled convulsively and moved from one to the other.

"He was called Willie," Sylvester said. "But he's your dog. We can call him any name you want."

For the next few days Penny tried several names but in exasperation she always ended with Willie. The dog answered to Willie. Joyce liked the dog. "I've nothing against him," she insisted. "He's a sweet dog. But Sylvester, this will prove to be impossible. The logistics of having a dog are impossible."

The trained puppy turned out to be less than half-trained. They put up infant's gates and kept him in the back hall when they were gone. He ate Joyce's plants, leaving only the stubby stalks. Sylvester took over the evening walks, because Penny should not be out wandering about that late. Scheduling became important. But after a month even Joyce admitted that the dog had done something for Penny. It gave her a companion, Sylvester knew.

Despite Joyce's objections, Willie abandoned the hall and began to sleep in Penny's room, starting the night on the floor but ending up on the bed. An only child needs a pet, Sylvester said. Sometimes it seemed to Joyce that comment was directed at her.

Summers they rented a house on the Cape. That very first year they argued over the dog. The man they usually rented from said no animals. No matter how well behaved. No animals. They had to find a new cottage. Joyce blamed Sylvester. By the end of the summer they had accepted the new place, it was farther from the beach, but pets were allowed. Sylvester said that the next summer, if Joyce wanted, they would put Willie in a kennel.

Penny, always an early-to-rise child, became, during her fifteenth year, a late sleeper. It became harder and harder to get her up. Then once up, a quick sip of coffee and she was ready to leave. She had slimmed down considerably. I'll be late! had become the new battle cry of the family. Joyce took over walking Willie in the morning. It was not the dog's fault. The animal should not be made to suffer.

Penny, Sylvester noted, was more and more outgoing. She joined the drama society in high school, and they saw her perform in three plays. In her senior year she had the lead in *The Importance of Being Earnest*. They went to the Russian Tea Room for a celebration dinner, and Sylvester and Joyce gave Penny a strand of cultured pearls. She had become a lovely girl.

Then came the flurry of college catalogues. Penny was going to study drama. At least, Joyce said, she's staying on the East Coast. Sylvester was astonished—college already. Joyce was wholehearted about the preparations. Sylvester was pleased, watching Joyce and Penny giggle together over magazines filled with going-to-college clothes. Willie began to pant, became apprehensive, and if a suitcase was left open or the trunk lid was up, he would immediately climb inside and settle himself on the folded clothes. Baby, Penny would say, and the dog would rush towards her, Penny embracing him.

What you don't realize, Sylvester told clients at lunch, is that the child goes off to college but the dog stays behind. He had a repertoire of Willie stories. He and Joyce felt sorry for the dog. For the first two weeks after Penny left, Willie slept in the hall facing the door. At night he could be heard prowling the apartment, he had never been separated from Penny before for any length of time. "Poor thing," Joyce would murmur. "I wish he could understand that the holidays will be here soon. She'll be back home again."

But not for Thanksgiving, and how they had waited for Thanksgiving. Penny was in the college infirmary with influenza. Sick and lonely, she was crying when Sylvester and Joyce drove up to be with her, boarding the dog with the vet for the weekend. The infirmary served Thanksgiving dinner but Penny couldn't eat. Joyce and Sylvester ate their own dinner at a local coffee shop—the featured Turkey Special.

"There must be somewhere," Sylvester said, "a hugely profitable gravy factory that produces this institutional glue. Smell it! I mean everywhere the odor is the same—not coincidence—a great institutional gravy pot exists."

Joyce wept quietly at the table.

They planned for Christmas then, a feast, presents, tickets to a good show. And Penny came home four days before

Christmas. When Willie saw her, his body quivered, and low throaty moans came from his chest. Penny dropped to her knees, and the dog washed her face with his tongue. Joyce and Sylvester just stood there. "Priorities," Sylvester said and smiled, he nudged Joyce.

At dinner Penny told them all about college life. Sylvester was surprised she had cut her hair. Penny hadn't mentioned that when they spoke on the telephone. The short hair made her look older.

The first morning Penny was home, Joyce dragged Sylvester out of bed, she put her finger to her lips to signal that he must be quiet, and led him to Penny's room. She pushed open the partially closed door. Sylvester stared at the bed. Willie was asleep in Penny's arms, his head buried in her shoulder. How young and vulnerable Penny and the dog looked.

There was a month of winter recess before Penny was due back at classes, but at the end of ten days she surprised Sylvester and Joyce by saying that she was going up to Vermont to go skiing with friends. They didn't even know that she knew how to ski. Penny hated sports. Now she laughed. I tried it out a couple of weekends, I seem to have a natural bent for it, she said. Joyce offered to buy her skis—other essentials. Penny said no. Her friend's family had plenty of stuff.

When Penny abandoned drama, Sylvester was not paying proper attention. There were problems at home. His fault, he knew. He had met the buyer for a small chain of women's specialty stores. She was newly divorced, in her late thirties, pretty, buoyant, witty. He had taken her to dinner several times. He made her a silver bracelet. She admired it extravagantly, but never once said it was an artistic creation. Sylvester respected her for that. It would be an affair soon, he realized. Joyce had begun to notice. It was in the middle of all this that Penny came home, unexpectedly arriving one March afternoon with one small suitcase. Penny had let her hair grow into a wild tangle of curls, she wore dangling gold earrings, long cotton skirts.

"What you look like," Joyce said angrily, "is a cheap imitation of a Gypsy."

"I'm sorry," Penny said, sitting in the living room absently petting Willie, "but your disappointment is not mine. I've got to give life a chance. I have no interest in school."

"Listen," Sylvester said, "you don't know what you're talking about."

Penny stared at him. "My opinions," she said, "are my opinions."

Neither Joyce nor Sylvester was able to dissuade her. It was her junior year—a year and a half to graduation. The young man Ted they met only briefly. The two of them were going to California to build something. The closest Penny came to softening was when she bade Willie good-bye. "I love you, Willie," she said. "I'll send for him when I settle."

Joyce never gave Sylvester an ultimatum. It was never her or me. It was simply that she got up one Saturday morning and said to Sylvester, "I would like you to leave, please." She was wearing a grey quilted robe, looking pale and disheveled.

"The politeness of it all," Sylvester said sarcastically. "We are so polite."

Joyce smiled. "If you prefer," she said. "Get the hell out of here!"

*   *   *

Sylvester moved into the buyer's apartment. The woman's name was Elaine. It was not a splendid affair. It turned out that she traveled most of the time, scurrying up and down the coast from Tampa to Boston. He was a stop-over. What he had to do was find his own place, which he located through one of his metal fittings suppliers just at the time he and Joyce decided to file for divorce. He sublet from a man who was going to Japan for two years. The apartment was reasonably close to Sylvester's office, he could stay healthy by walking to work.

He and Joyce had returned to civilized relations. Once in a while he had dinner with her, usually after she had heard from Penny. If he was invited to the apartment, Willie would become tremendously excited. Sylvester was disturbed to notice that the dog seemed to be putting on weight, but he said nothing.

Penny wrote infrequently. It was mostly Joyce who received the postcards with their cryptic mentions of men, always new names; she sent Daddy her love, hugs for Willie.

One day Joyce called Sylvester at his office. Her voice was happy. "I have a letter from Penny—a genuine letter," she said. "Sylvester, she's decided to go back to school—the letter has a return address. She has an apartment! She's enrolled in UCLA. Anthropology, she writes. She's studying anthropology."

They felt relieved, joyous, she wasn't lost, she had come back, it was all worthwhile then. Sylvester knew that he should ask Joyce out, they should celebrate, but he was busy working on his spring line and he had recently met a very attractive young woman.

*   *   *

The year Penny graduated, Sylvester, checking to make certain that Joyce had no similar plans, flew out to L.A., and stayed a week. "Penny looks fine," he told Joyce when he got back. He had invited Joyce for drinks and sushi. She was catching a train, giving a talk in Boston. They had a few hours.

"But how does she *seem*?" Joyce asked. Joyce had gone to see her in L.A. three years before. Penny had said that emotionally she wasn't ready to come back East even for a visit.

"A bit heavier," Sylvester said. "Plans all made, though. Already enrolled in graduate school."

"And a man?" Joyce said. "I presume there's a man."

"Yes," Sylvester said, "a man is living in the apartment—a graduate student."

"You don't approve of this one," Joyce said. "I can hear that in your voice."

"He's all right," Sylvester said. "Nothing wrong with him—about her age I guess. Hard to know. I found him rather self-absorbed, a touch stolid."

Actually, both the man and Penny had bored the hell out of him the entire week.

Sylvester broke up with the girl named Madeleine the very month it became definite that the building where he now lived was going co-op. He didn't want to buy. He wasn't fond of living there. The question was, where to go? He had been toying with the idea of taking a year's sabbatical. Just closing up his business temporarily and going away, but that was fiscally dangerous. Customers were fickle, forgot you instantly.

Joyce called up and invited him to dinner. Come up to the apartment, she said, if you don't mind. Sylvester didn't mind. He selected a bottle of good burgundy and went. Willie barked on seeing him, a nervous sound. The black spots around his muzzle had sprouted grey hairs.

"Hush," Joyce said to the dog. "Hey hush."

"Hi old boy," Sylvester said, patting Willie, scratching him behind the ears. "How you doing, old fellow?"

"Open the wine," Joyce said. "Food's almost ready."

Sylvester waited patiently through the meal, he knew that Joyce must have a reason for inviting him. He listened to her conversation about her work, about her papers, about her successes in her department, she had taken an academic position.

"I have a monstrous request," she said finally, offering espresso in tiny cups with anisette and slivers of orange peel. "I will understand if you refuse, but I felt I had to ask."

"Shoot," Sylvester said.

"I'm going into the hospital," she said.

His heart pounded.

She raised her hand. "Not terrible, not fatal. A hysterectomy but nothing malignant—it just must be. And afterwards, I would like to go down to Fort Lauderdale to my sister's to convalesce, to recoup. With the hospital and the trip—we're talking about six weeks—maybe two months tops. The truth of it is—there's Willie. He's no young pup, you know. I could use the kennel like I do when there's a meeting or something. But two months—at his age—I don't know if he could survive."

Sylvester nodded.

"It's outrageous, I know," she said. "But could you possibly take him?"

The dog, hearing his name, had moved restlessly around the table. Sylvester looked down at him—a sweet, loyal dog. "You know how I feel about Willie. There's my apartment, though." Sylvester said. "No dogs, Joyce. Anyway, I'm planning to leave there. I'm looking right now. Otherwise I'd take him in a minute."

She hesitated. "Here," she said. "You could stay here. I mean if you're looking, I'll be away. I pay the doormen to walk Willie in the middle of the day. I do mornings and evenings—but for a few bucks more I'm certain they'll do the other walks too."

Here? Sylvester thought about it. He could leave his apartment, spend two months looking for a new place. He would certainly be comfortable in this apartment. "If the logistics can be worked out," he said. "I'll do it. And I don't mind the morning and evening walks—probably need the exercise."

They shook hands and agreed to discuss it further.

Sylvester sent over an embarrassing load of boxes. Stacked in Joyce's hall, they looked worse than they had in his apartment. Most of the furniture had been sold, but he was left with this. It's all right, Joyce soothed, anyway I won't be here to look at them. He had arrived the night before she was due to go to the hospital. It was the best he could manage. He slept that night in Penny's old room, on her bed. He was conscious of Joyce sleeping just across the hall, he thought he felt or heard her breathing. He wondered what would happen if he got up and crossed the hall. But he didn't dare, there had been no overtures, no expectations. He fell asleep.

He offered to stay home from the office the next morning and drive Joyce to the hospital. It's not necessary, she said. I'm not feeling like an invalid yet. Sylvester kissed her cheek. He would visit, he said. She nodded. Willie accompanied her to the door, saw that a walk with him wasn't planned, and returned to Sylvester's side.

Penny called during the week Joyce was in the hospital. "It's going just fine," he told her on the telephone, "nothing to worry about. Your mother is doing swimmingly well."

"Thank you, Daddy," Penny said.

Willie, wagging his tail, greeted Sylvester every morning. Sylvester would put on an old sweat shirt and pants and take the dog out for a walk. It was something of a pain, a drag. But Joyce had been doing it all these years, he shouldn't complain. The dog was getting old, he realized. A bit arthritic. He never jumped on Sylvester's bed. Sylvester had abandoned Penny's room for the master bedroom; there was, after all, a television in that room, and the bed was larger. He established a routine, the morning walk, the evening walk, the necessity for always checking to see that there was dog food. Willie was appreciative. Sometimes Sylvester thought he caught him sniffing around the bedroom as if on a hunt. Searching for Joyce, was he? Nevertheless, Willie was a warm companion.

Joyce didn't return to the apartment from the hospital. Sylvester offered his assistance, and this time she accepted. Despite his protests, she asked him to drive her directly to the airport, and she left for Florida.

Sylvester marked it down to curiosity, to concern, but he was ashamed of himself. He looked through the desk drawers, he read Joyce's letters. There was someone named Harold. He sent letters from many different places. There was an extensive correspondence with a Kenneth, but that seemed to be chiefly professional. There were other, more cryptic signs. He was also glad to see that Joyce was doing all right financially, she had never given that enough attention before. She had investments, some stock, and her income was adequate. Although he wasn't legally obligated, there had been no alimony requested—just child support. Still, he felt responsible—he would never have let Joyce starve. But he needn't worry, he could see that she was all right.

After six weeks Joyce called him. "How's everything?" she said.

"Fine," he said.

"Willie?"

"Fit," he said. "Fine."

She spoke about the weather. "The thing is," she said finally, "would it be possible—would I be a terrible stinker—if I stayed another two weeks?"

"No," he said. He hadn't even started looking for an apartment, but he didn't say that. "The pup and I can easily hold down the fort."

"Thank you, Sylvester," she said. "I really appreciate it."

The woman he had been dating, the sister of one of his clients, found him an apartment in Washington Heights. He paid a premium for it, but it was decent. He had the place painted and then ordered a truck to pick up his boxes. He figured it best that he move out before Joyce arrived. She had his new address, and the superintendent accepted a package from UPS. Joyce had sent him a case of Florida oranges.

He made certain that Joyce's apartment was clean, vacuumed up the dog hair, stocked the refrigerator, checked the dog food supply. Joyce arrived at seven in the evening. She arrived by taxi, and she looked tanned and rested. Sylvester kissed her warmly.

"You look great," he said.

"Thank you," she said.

He saw her quickly examining the apartment. "I'm going to let you get unpacked and settled," he said. "I'll call you later."

"You've been wonderful," Joyce said. "You know I mean that."

"My pleasure," Sylvester said, and waved good-bye.

Willie, a constant of love, accompanied him to the door, and then, becoming aware that Sylvester was not carrying a leash, turned around and, without a backward glance, trotted down the hall to Joyce.

Lists and Categories

~~~~~~~~~~

I wasn't about to put myself in the hands of some jerk. I can tell you what I'm not suffering from—I am not suffering from a brain tumor, the punch-drunk syndrome, heat-stroke, or peripheral nerve damage. Who would believe my score on the Wechsler Adult Intelligence Scale? Makes me a super underachiever. However, I deserve credit for having recognized that I needed assistance—all right, emotional help—that's going a long way. But I didn't jump in. I investigated—looked up the crowd of potential helpers. Checked their credentials, their societies, their certification. All of this I accomplished before I selected.

Lucy—God, am I sick of first names—says, I can help you. She has written articles. *Life as Polymorphous Passive Fear. Protective Behavior and Its Affinities.* First time I sit in her office the secretary gives me this clipboard with a form to fill out. It goes beyond Blue Cross numbers.

Describe the nature of your maladjustment to modern life?

"We hate him," they said.

I stared at my two little lollipops. They were eight and ten, and this was the first time I had ever been able to get them into matching outfits. Until then, similar clothing had always emphasized the disturbing contrast between Audrey's slim dark looks and Eleanor's chubby squatness. But now, ever since she turned ten, Eleanor had dropped a lot of fat. So two cherubs in blue denim. Two princesses from Lord & Taylor. Also, they were almost friends. They had been friends for six months.

"No," I said firmly, but smiling. "You do not hate him. He is your Daddy."

Was I comforted to hear that they were on my side? Certainly. Even though it was wrong, and I wouldn't let them get away with it. Why shouldn't they hate him? Let them.

"We do so," Eleanor said.

"Yes," Audrey said, although not really a chorus. She was never a chorus.

"He left you," Eleanor said. "He left you for someone else."

The influences of modern life—would I have known such facts at her age? What had I known at age ten? —Probably everything.

"He did not leave me for someone else," I said. "We are happier apart." That was so. At least about our being happier apart. There wasn't someone else—there were *someones* else.

Eleanor picked up her glass of chocolate milk and sipped greedily. Audrey hadn't touched hers. "He did," she said. "You know he did. Listen, we know. They leave for someone else."

"You know from television, I suppose, Miss Smarty?"

"From everybody," Audrey said.

She was eight.

"We made a list," Eleanor said.

I died, my heart stopped, I trembled. Had they made a list? Of their daddy's women? Could they have?

"This is a list," Eleanor said, "of everybody we know who split."

"I put down some of the names," Audrey said.

"We made it up with Carol and Wendy—the three of us."

"The four of us," Audrey said.

"Lists," I said, trying to turn the conversation, "are for shopping. And that's what I thought we would do this afternoon. Visit the stores, have a drugstore lunch—the kind you like, then maybe a movie."

"The list," Eleanor said coldly, "took us all day. Everyone we knew, and relatives—ours, Carol's, Wendy's. We used names from dancing school, we did Girl Scouts, we did from Wendy's mother's exercise class, from Dramatics Club, from Carol's stupid therapy group. The only rule was that you had to know the person or have heard about them firsthand. Otherwise it wasn't fair. We have two hundred thirty-seven names."

"What?"

"Two-three-seven," Audrey said, "in three columns."

"That doesn't sound right," Eleanor said, "sounds like we put the names in three columns. Actually, the first column was girl, the next column was boy, the next column was third person—person left for."

"And you knew," I said, "you *knew*, did you, who it was the person left for? Just like that—clean and neat."

"Sure," Eleanor said. "I mean, Grandma left Joe for George. Grandpa left Grandma for Dorothy. You could have two names in the third column, if necessary."

"But you had to write real small," Audrey said. "They wouldn't let me put any of the names down."

"You write like a baby," Eleanor said, "all scrawls and loops."

"Do not!"

Have you attempted to solve your problems?

Neal was a Play Therapist. He was a doctor, he was a psychiatrist. He said he was a Play Therapist. We were there because Audrey had pulled her pants down in class and lifted her skirt. Eleanor, our other daughter, as far as we knew, hadn't done anything. We were in big trouble, the Play Therapist said. I wore a navy blue suit. Took me all morning to dress. My hands were significantly cold. Raoul, the Daddy, was there. I told the Play Therapist to invite him. I can't call, I said. Not even for my baby.

In truth, I knew that Raoul would have shown up if I had called. But think of the greater effect if the summons came from Neal the Play Therapist.

We sat in the beige room. I had been to the offices of Child Behavior before. There was an institutional cum schoolroom, a warm maple-inspired office, and there was the beige room. In the beige room Neal liked to talk modern.

"Just how liberal would you say you are?" he asked. He was smiling. I could have used a little wrath.

"Not liberal at all," I said.

"Ever make love in front of your girls?"

Raoul took a deep breath. "Are you crazy?" he said.

Neal smiled. "Did I say that was necessarily bad? Do they see you with others?"

We both shook our heads.

"But it is my fault," Raoul said. "I know it's my fault. I am at fault. I have hurt my babies."

I did not look at him.

"Many people get divorced," Neal said.

"Most," I said.

"We aren't divorced," Raoul said.

We will be, I think.

Raoul began to cry, he wiped his eyes, he blew his nose. "If you knew," he said, "how much I love my little girls. Should I move back?" He allowed his voice to tremble.

"If possible," Neal said. "For the time."

They both looked at me.

I was the wronged party.

Daddy had walked out.

"For the girls," I said.

We were in Family Therapy once a week, both girls went to Play Therapy twice a week. Raoul sold the car, taught a class at night, I increased my typing speed. One day, in exhaustion and despair, we started sleeping together.

The question I ought to have asked Neal, perhaps at the beginning, was should I have spanked Audrey. You do that again, my mother would have said, and I'll break both your legs.

What part has your family played in your decision to come here?

I called my brother one day. "Sylvester," I said, "let's have lunch?"

We didn't have to discuss it—either it would be on a weekday or no day. It's not that I didn't like his wife, Joyce. I couldn't take her.

"We ought do this more often," I said. We had steak sandwiches. The food was rich and sweetly greasy.

"How you been?" Sylvester said.

We smiled at each other. He is three, four years older. A tall sturdy person.

"Actually," I said, wiping my lips with a napkin, staring at the purple smear. Joyce never wore dark-colored lipsticks. Joyce was distinctly pale. "I thought I might ask a bit of advice. Share my problems, so to speak."

Sylvester didn't look pleased.

"Divorce," I said. "Me and Raoul."

Sylvester clicked his teeth. "Too bad," he said. "In truth, Cissie—the way it is—I mean, I don't feel I am equipped to give advice. Think a moment, were we close? You and I, were we?"

"You're my brother," I said.

"I don't mean that. I would always help you if you needed it—but besides money—I wouldn't know what to give you—certainly not advice."

"Of course we were close," I said. "We *are* close."

Sylvester shook his head. "I don't recall being close to anyone from the time I was a kid. All this nostalgia for simple family life that's going around. I mean, none of us were close—you, me, Mother, Father. The only family in which I saw that intimacy—were some people I knew when I was a kid. Now *they* were close. But I suspect we follow in the paths of our parents—for instance, how close are you to your kids?"

"I love them."

"I love my daughter too. But does she know what I think, what I feel, me as a person?—No way. Closeness may be a myth."

Describe your outside life—apart from the family?

Eleanor and Audrey had come home for Thanksgiving weekend. Eleanor was sitting in the living room reading the newspaper when her sister came into the room, slamming the front door, bringing a pleasing chill into the overheated room. Audrey was a pretty girl with short, well-cut hair and good spirits. She was no longer the sullen teenager. The sisters had fought so often, but time had eased that. Audrey was a sophomore at City College, she was awaiting the future. She had come to terms with the present, it was just a brief stop. It made her tolerant.

"Everyone still asleep?" Audrey asked.

"Mother is," Eleanor said. "Daddy went out I think."

Audrey threw her coat across the couch and flopped down beside it. "Guess who Daddy's got an eye for?"

"Who?" Eleanor said.

"The Disco Princess."

"What?"

"Come on," Audrey said. "You haven't been away that long. You know who I mean—that cummerbund bunny?"

Eleanor lowered her newspaper. "They still live here?"

"Sure," Audrey said. "Daddy watches her from a front window." Audrey made a dramatic gesture, reaching back and pulling the sheer curtains away from the window. "He watches her coming and going. And there is plenty of coming and going."

Eleanor was amused. Audrey smiled back.

Eleanor searched for her name. "Michelle," she said triumphantly.

"No, it was Miche*lline*. An eye makeup name."

"That's the one."

"She always made good watching."

"Daddy watches her," Audrey said. "He doesn't know I know, but he does." Audrey giggled. She stood up. "It's the walk," she said. "That exaggerated, can-I-make-it-to-the-curb walk. Such high heels, what a magnificently deformed spine she must have."

These are my baby girls. They are engaged in conversation in the living room. How do I know? The room is bugged. The intercom for the door. If I turn on the central control—I can hear everything. All the rooms are bugged. When I go out, I connect a tape recorder.

You think I'm worried about the Disco Princess? She's the real thing, though. She doesn't overdo it. Maybe the girls are jealous. The Disco Princess never dresses up in costumes or puts a streak of purple in her hair like some I could name. She has the profile of Sephardic royalty. As soon as it grows dark, they come—the big cars to take her to anonymous halls in New Rochelle or Yonkers, where she wiggles under strobe lights and struts to sounds. She is breaking her mother's heart.

What do I think? I think one day the Disco Princess will go chunky and get herself married in some barn of a catering hall that resembles a disco only minus the lights and the darkest people.

Meanwhile, Daddy looks.

I have enrolled in school. It is fashionable for adult women to go back to school. What am I going to be? I am studying many things. Debating and choosing. Maybe I'll be a nurse, maybe a social worker. Teaching is out. My patience with kids is over. Can you imagine!—I once wanted six.

When Eleanor and Audrey were little ones, clinging to

my hand, I was their best friend. I never lost either one of
them in a department store.

Raoul, their daddy, got a fellowship to England. Twelve
months with the entire family or six months alone. He
flipped a coin. Who won? The pisser went off like a flash.
Did he write? Elegies of words—sonnets of advice—a
travelogue of far away. Ancient stones, he said. I am
walking ancient stones.

The Elgin Marbles, he haikued. I saw them.

The kids were in school. I did free-lance typing, I owned
my own IBM. I hunted for companionship—not clubs, I
had a headache full of clubs. There are stories about house-
wives and the afternoon dalliance. Where do they find the
men? Answer advertisements? I'm not looking for diseases.

Then one afternoon Mrs. Disco Princess is shopping, I
see her leave dragging a wire cart behind her, a tangle of
wheels, runners in her stockings. I trot across the street.
Should I borrow coffee or sugar? Coffee sounds better.

The Disco Princess answers the door. It is eleven o'clock,
she is without makeup. I could even have awakened her.

"Yes," she says.

Does she know me?

"Cissie," I say. "A neighbor—I know your mother, I
met your mother once. I wonder—could I borrow some
coffee? Even instant."

The Disco Princess looks older than I would have
guessed.

"I made some," she says. "Come in. Have a cup."

"Great," I say.

Her mother's kitchen is better-looking than mine—
everything a cheerful yellow, everything shining. It's what
I've always said—appearance tells nothing. Did that woman
look like a lot of shine?

We sit on stools and the Disco Princess pours me a mug of coffee.

"I'm beat," she says.

"You dance a lot," I say. No point in evading the fact.

"Every night," she says.

"Fun?"

"Sometimes," she says.

Any moment now I can spring away. One quick movement. "At those places where you dance," I say, "everyone young?"

"Yes," she says. "At my places, yes."

Michelline telephones me. Call, I have warned her, between nine and four. No chance of it being nine, she says. Bank on noon. She has made a date for me. Can I dance? I have practiced with the television. Wear heavy makeup, she says. But it will be dark. Will the man guess that I am his age? I went shopping for a dress. My dress sparkles. It is not especially nice. In the morning mail I get an essay about a boat ride on the Thames.

The way it works is this. The baby-sitter arrives, I abandon the kids to her care. I'm wrapped in a raincoat, hair under a scarf. I trot to the corner, walk two blocks to where the Disco Princess and escorts wait. The truth of the matter is that I am having a good time.

The Disco Princess connects me with Herman. Herman has experience. My first five girls, he tells me, were black. He tells me about some new girls—about Nea, about Marie, about Delores, about Bebe. We make love in the backseat of the limousine, and that makes me giggle.

The Rolling Stones have separated, the Disco Princess says. And what's up with Sonny and Cher?

I give the Disco Princess two record albums for her birthday. To my surprise, she is twenty-eight.

I buy a silver dress, also a gold one. I have a rainbow of scarves.

You're breaking my heart, I hear Mrs. Disco Princess scream one morning.

The Stones have definitely separated, ditto Sonny and Cher, also people I know very well. What I want, I tell the Disco Princess, is a lover with staying power, a terrific-looking man.

"Don't we all," she says.

Raoul came back. It was no longer safe so I gave up my life with the Disco Princess. I could tell by the light in Raoul's eyes, by the ardent nature of his embraces, that somewhere he also had a good time.

The Disco Princess and I have nodded at each other occasionally in the drugstore, in the supermarket, at the bus stop. Still, I consider her a friend. Even though ten years have gone by, I regard the Disco Princess as my friend. She would not do anything with Raoul.

I mean, in daylight you can tell that she is now thirty-eight.

So when's the wedding?

Describe the nature of your current thoughts.

I've become part of the corporate world, full time. It's not a bad job. It gets me up and dressed every day. In Grand Central, in the light of Information, I bump into a friend. He is basically a friend of Raoul's. We have lunch together. Our friendship grows.

I suspect that Audrey and Eleanor have seen us. Did they tell their daddy?

That's it, Raoul says.

You can't have your cake and eat it too.

In my first session with my therapist, Lucy, I show her a picture of Raoul. "From his expression," she says, "I can tell everything—I have character profiles of men like him. Get rid of the bum."

At last, a definitive answer.

Orphans

～～～～～

I'm involved with craziness, concerned about craziness, craziness is eating me up. Aren't my decisions my own? The reason I am seeing another therapist is because of a promise. The promise was to see a therapist. Before I did something *crazy*. The implication being that any action— pardon me—any extreme action must be crazy. What am I planning to do? Slit my throat, rape a young boy, move to California? I am planning to have a face-lift—minor surgery. My friends—God bless them—called my brother. My brother! Sylvester, they said, do something with her. They might just as well have called my last husband. And *he* is not the reason for the surgery. Try telling that to friends. Wait, they advise. Look in the mirror. You look great. And because craziness begets craziness my brother came to see me, but he, of course, had already forgotten the pleas of my friends.

It is fall. The trees look good. I have held my job for fourteen months. It is Saturday, it is eleven o'clock in the morning, my brother Sylvester sits at my kitchen table. My apartment is on East Twenty-third Street. All night a drunk yelled beneath my windows. The apartment is conveniently located, you can go anywhere in New York from Twenty-third Street. I am wearing my old pink chenille robe, I look terrible. I don't care. If you invite yourself over for coffee on Saturday morning, expect nothing. Sylvester brought the *Times* with him, he brought a bag of bagels, he brought a choice of three kinds of Danish. Clearly he felt guilty about arriving this way.

"There could have been a man here," I said.

"I called," Sylvester said. He watched me make the coffee.

"You called from downstairs—you called on the intercom for God's sake. That is not calling."

"You could have said don't come up."

"To you—with the voice of doom coming up through the tube, running past the roaches—how?"

"The thing is," Sylvester said, pushing back his chair, tapping an uneven rhythm on the table, "I really believe that if I were under ultraviolet light it would read *Get him!* on my forehead. Is there a God? Of course, there must be, and when the time is right, he reads what it says on my forehead and acts accordingly. Everything was going great, swimmingly great. My fall line of jewelry is selling. And I have a piece or two that I'm really proud of for a change. Also, I am seriously thinking of remarrying. This Charlotte—you have to meet her—is uncommonly decent. Then Dad calls."

My heart sank. Our father lived uptown, he lived in the Bronx. Who saw him? Nevertheless, my heart sank. "He's sick? Out of money?"

"No," Sylvester said. "He personally is fine. It's Dorothy—Dorothy is sick."

My last husband kept telling me I'm a child of divorce. It does things to you, he said. There are effects. Maybe so. But I do not consider myself a child of divorce. An adult of divorce perhaps. That made my husband angry. Another thing that made that husband angry was a clock we bought in Amsterdam. This clock has two metal circles with arcane signs, the metal circles turn, one left, one right. The red circle is for minutes, the black, hours. Is it easy to tell time with this clock? No. My husband hated that clock. Stupid machinery, he said. I offered to take the clock to my office.

I like Dorothy. "That's too bad," I said.

"Dad says who can he turn to if not his son. He says—forgive me—that his daughter hardly knows he's alive."

"Great," I said, pulling tighter the belt of my robe. "I owe him? Tell me, what do I owe him? Anyway, is it your responsibility—Dorothy is not *our* mother."

"That's unkind," Sylvester said. "Dorothy is a decent person. She was never the Other Woman."

"All right—that's true."

"The trouble is—Dad thinks Dorothy is bonkers," Sylvester said.

"God," I said. "He's going to put her away. Can't afford another divorce. He's going to put her away!"

"No, no," Sylvester said. "It's not that. Not that at all. He's worried, really worried. We made a date for lunch at the Second Avenue Deli. Dad looks good, prosperous, though his suit is too pale for the season. What I'm going to do is wait—I'm going to wait until he tells me the reason for the lunch. In the meantime we consume pastrami on rye, three pickles apiece, and bottles of Dr. Brown's cream. Dorothy, Dad says finally, is causing me a touch of trouble. I watched Dad closely, I calculated that he had been married at least fourteen years, the alimony would be high.

"She's not an old woman, our father says. Dorothy is younger than me. But sometimes, I think she is becoming senile, sometimes I think a nervous breakdown. The truth is, Sylvester, she acts dopey all the time.

"We sat in silence. I drank the rest of my soda. On my plate were crumbs of black pepper, a scum of fat, two crusts. How dopey? I finally ask. Hard to say, Dad says. What I'm requesting is a short conversation between you and her. She's fond of you, Sylvester. You'll talk.

"What exactly are you worried about? I ask. Our father stares past me at his reflection in a mirror. She's nuts, he says. She gets up at night. I don't hear, I'm a heavy sleeper. But last week I woke up—I went to piss. She was kneeling on the floor by the windowsill, white night-gown, bare feet. Christ, I almost jumped out of my skin. Dorothy, I said, what the hell? She didn't answer. I thought she was sick. I thought she had a stroke. Tante Elena had such a stroke, sitting in an armchair one day, she stiffened.

"What did Dorothy say afterwards? I ask. How did she explain this? She says nothing, Dad says and coughs. She stands up, smiles, and goes back to bed. And sometimes— we're having dinner or watching television—she gets up and walks away—just like that, midfork so to speak."

I sighed. "Another woman, Sylvester? It sounds like she found out about another woman."

Sylvester nodded. "That's what I thought. I asked him. You're playing around, isn't that it? What do you mean? our Dad snorts. You're telling me I'm responsible for the craziness going on in her head? Possibly, I say. Did she see you? You never were careful.

"See me? he says. See me doing what? The most—I say the most—was sitting in a restaurant too close to home and talking with someone. Perhaps a hand on her arm. I'm not apologizing. I love Dorothy.

"We stared at each other—Dad and me. Anyway, Dad said, I don't think that's it. I want you to go and talk to her, Sylvester.

"I didn't want to—but I said yes."

"I took the subway. They still live off Mosholu Parkway. Dorothy answered the door. What did I do? I sniffed her breath. No alcohol. She kissed my cheek. Sylvester, she said. Welcome, Sylvester. I gave her a bouquet of red rosebuds, I bought them before I took the subway, they were fresh. I also brought a large bag of pistachio nuts.

"Dorothy went to get a vase. I watched her. She looked bad, thin, pale. How's everything? I said. Dorothy smiled. So-so, she said.

"We sat down. I was trying to start. Thinking of a beginning question. Your father asked you to talk to me, Dorothy said suddenly. I had my opening. I immediately decided against lying. He said you were peaked looking. He said I was nuts, she said. I shook my head. I denied it. He could be right, Sylvester, Dorothy said. But I don't think so. I'm trying to reach something. What? I asked. A vision, she said. It was religion then—or yoga. Not so bad. Nothing wrong with that, I thought.

"Dorothy smiled. When I was eleven years old, Dorothy said, there came a long summer. I know what you are thinking, but this was a longer summer than usual. My friends Sydney and Catherine—we wanted to do something, to call attention. It started because we were bored. We had a private game. We were vacationing on a small farm, three families.

"It was a working farm. There were woods behind the house where we went to play, watching out for snakes, wild animals. I am certain it was Sydney who invented the game of visions. It wouldn't have been me. I would have been afraid. I thought of God as wrathful. We picked Catherine to have the vision, she tanned poorly, looked pale. Do it like a holy picture, Sydney ordered. Catherine knelt. We developed a ritual. Catherine would clasp her hands and declare she saw something. That was as far as we could go at first. But later we got better.

"The farmer's wife saw us. Anyone else and we would have been scolded—sent back to the house. But she thought it was real. Thought we were *holy*. Suddenly there was moaning, howling, babbling. We were frightened. We ran to our parents. Too late. Visions, my father said, I'll give you visions.

"Dorothy stares at me. I think something was there, Sylvester, she said. Playacting, I said. Dorothy shakes her head. I think Catherine saw something. I think it was an important time and there were signs. We just misinterpreted them. It's because you're tired, maybe nostalgic, I said. Honest, Dorothy, that's all it is. Dorothy sighed. Anyway, she said, don't worry, I've decided to give up remembering."

"You think it's settled," Sylvester asked me, "or was she just trying to get rid of me?"

"Settled," I said. "Sounds settled to me."

He looked at me. "By the way," he said, remembering why he came. "What's this stuff about a face-lift? Aren't you ashamed of yourself—here we are *facing* maybe a real crisis. Just think about that next time."

That was it—was the choice of words intentional? *Facing* a crisis. Might he have added you are meshugah, tetched, loco? Trust Sylvester to upset me, and then go away, leaving me alone in my apartment. I dialed a telephone number. I put a handkerchief over the receiver to disguise my voice. He answered the telephone, I think I woke my father up.

"Spend more time with her," I whispered. "Drop everyone else—or God will punish you."

I have plenty of my own problems. But you can't get rid of friends.

"I'm not going to horn in on your celebration," I told Imelda. "The man is going away. Why would he want me along on your last dinner?"

"That's just it," Imelda said. "I don't want it to be like a *last* dinner. I want it to be more casual. I'm not giving him up, you realize. This is just temporary."

I sighed. Imelda was hard to discourage.

I took my Persian lamb with the chinchilla collar out of storage. What were we celebrating? Marsh had been made a regional manager. And so young. He had gone out to Calgary to scout around.

He told me what happened. We were drinking champagne cocktails. On Wednesday, he called Imelda. Come, he said. She took the girl and the boys and flew out. They were staying in a hotel. The company was helping Marsh get established. "She didn't like it," Marsh said.

"I hated it," Imelda said. "I took a bus ride. Marsh said damn the bus ride. I rode all over town. It reminds me of

home, Cissie. I can imagine how cold it must be, all those
narrow houses, those houses squeezing together, hud-
dling on the prairies for warmth. I hate it. Who needs it?
I miss the city. I could not stay."

The parting, they agreed, would be temporary. Marsh
would settle, then they would see. "Life," Marsh said, "is
the same everywhere. You think it isn't, but it is. Once
you find your way, it's the same."

Still, the evening was probably successful. Marsh
took turns dancing with each of us. I could see what
Imelda had in mind. It did have the air of a man leaving
on a business trip—even if an extended one. At one
point Imelda tried to be subtle. "Look at Cissie," she
said to Marsh. "Isn't she beautiful? Doesn't she look
youthful."

"Sure thing," Marsh said. "Time to go, girls. Ready,
set, everyone *face* left."

Imelda had a job, she never thought of it as a career. She
was part of a decision-making team. Marsh used to brag
that you could support a family on her salary. She could
still afford to keep the apartment. Not too much for her
at all. The other dividing was hard. The boys were twelve
and fourteen. They were city boys, sharp-tongued, careful. They played baseball. Imelda laughed, because that
was how she defined them. They played baseball. On
Saturdays they went to the park with Marsh. At the
dinner table they discussed the top-ranked teams, the best
coaches, the eccentricities of players.

The boys wanted to go with Marsh. It wasn't that they
didn't love their mother. They loved her. But they would
miss Marsh more than they could bear. It was terrible,
Imelda told me. The apartment was a waterfall—a salty

river. I feel as if an onion is in front of me at all times, she said.

There was no question about Emily going. Emily was seventeen. But before her brothers left, she hugged them, she kissed them, she admonished them. Behave, she said. "My home is here, Aunt Cissie," she said to me. She is my godchild. Sometimes, I think we are very close.

The apartment was rent-stabilized. It would be foolish to give it up, Imelda said, even if it was big for two. There were three bedrooms. Imelda wouldn't have touched the boys' bedroom, but Marsh wanted the furniture shipped. The boys need the old, he said, the familiar. The room was empty then. Imelda couldn't stand that. She turned the room into a den, bought a couch covered with a red and black plaid wool. The couch opened into a bed at a touch. She put a large television in one corner of the room.

I was having dinner with Imelda. Old friends mean everything. "My divorce," I told Imelda, "is coming through." She nodded and hugged me.

"It's for the best," she said.

"How are the kids?" I asked.

"Marsh and I speak once a week. I think the boys' voices quiver on the telephone. But I don't know, maybe I'm *looking* for it. They don't admit to unhappiness."

In spring it was clear that Imelda was nervous, insomniac, anorectic. She did not want to go to Calgary for a visit. She did not feel fit enough to mind the boys in the city. Marsh and the boys were going backpacking. Emily flew to Calgary to join them.

The three weeks alone were good for Imelda. We went to dinner together. Then she was busy. I guessed. "You've met someone?" I said.

Imelda giggled. "Douglas," she said. Not exactly a client, but a business connection. Douglas was separated from his wife. "Guilt is funny," Imelda said. "First I thought of opening the couch into a bed. But the other bed was *my* bed—it was no longer the marriage bed."

At Christmas the boys came East. Imelda and I took everyone to Radio City for the annual show. Where were my daughters? With friends, I told Imelda. With friends. Imelda's boys were certainly polite. They had a good time, but the oldest, now almost sixteen, said that he did not want to live in this city. Too big, he said.

The boys missed the next Easter in New York. Imelda was upset. She listened to Marsh's explanation. It wasn't her, he said. It was skiing. They had taken up skiing. Their team was traveling during the spring vacation to where the mountains were the best. You ought to see them, Marsh said. Birds, flying birds.

One day Imelda's youngest brother called her from Milwaukee. I think you have to come out, he told her. I believe it's all over with Mother. "I'll pay for your ticket," Imelda said to me. "But I just cannot go alone." I didn't know what to say, what excuse to make. So Imelda and I flew to Wisconsin. Her brother met us at the airport. We shook hands.

Their mother lived in a run-down building. The rooms smelled, a fetid closed-in smell, breeding on itself. The woman looked dazed, her hair badly combed.

The doctor made the arrangements. Imelda insisted on riding in the ambulance. At the nursing home they put her mother in a bed with the sides up, high metal bars painted pale green.

For a moment, her mother stared at Imelda, really stared.

Was she crazy?

Imelda and I went to speak to the nurse. The nurse patted Imelda's arm. "No one is crazy all the time," she said. "Life must be *faced*."

I'm not vain, I have only the normal desire to be attractive. Girls today can be themselves. Didn't I say that to my daughters? Different, I said, when I was growing up. Everyone wanted to be pretty. My daughters stared at me, sullen, disinterested. They were seventeen and fifteen at the time. The truth was that they were pretty. They were quite pretty, so what did it matter that I told them to be themselves.

I had my appendix out five years ago. They put me in a room with a woman having a hernia operation. Mornings she creamed her neck and throat for an hour, she repeated the act every evening. She dieted, she said, all the time. Take care of yourself, she warned. I turned away from her. You'll regret it, she said, just look at me.

My daughter Audrey keeps calling. You don't need a face-lift, she says. You are only forty-nine. Accept the divorce, mother. My daughters don't live at home anymore. Eleanor has four children, all boys, and lives in Santa Fe with her husband, who is an accountant. I visited her after the birth of her third boy. We went to fast-food places to eat, we would pull in and stop our car at the spot where you press a button. Order please? the voice would say. We would say what we wanted. Then a girl in red shorts skated over and attached a tray to our window. We went to drive-in movies and saw films whose titles I cannot recall. In the backseat the boys whimpered in their sleep. We sat the three of us, Eleanor, the accountant, and me squeezed together. There was always salt on my fingers from the popcorn.

My best friends Claire Anne, Imelda, and Bernadette are dubious. Bad timing, they insist. My therapist is named Dora. We are going back through my life. From her I have not yet received a yes or no to the face-lift. She and I have differing although not incompatible views. She is big on small traumas, I do large ones. My father lives in the city, I tell her, with his second wife. My mother is dead.

I have blown up the last photograph of my mother, probably her best. She is wearing a tailored blouse and her hair is smooth and turned under at the ends. I have the picture in a silver frame. She looks good. I have observed some of the mothers of my friends. Claire Anne resembles her mother. Her mother lives here in the city, they see each other frequently. Claire Anne's mother is in her mid-seventies. On her cheeks are the folds, the loosening flesh of old age.

In truth, I am being realistic. How will I look when I get old? I have no model before me. How would I know what my mother looked like when she was old—she was never old. A face-lift is practical—I know what I look like today. With a face-lift, I postpone the unknown. What does it have to do with divorce? It has nothing to do with divorce. One day my therapist says to me, "You must *face* facts."

That's it.

I select my plastic surgeon with care. He must be Board Certified. I know what I am about. I ask professional questions. The doctors I have interviewed are impressed.

Not many patients take the time, they say. Is that crazy? Being careful.

Claire Anne's mother had one finger under my chin and she used an authoritative voice to make me swivel my head from one side to the other. "This way," she'd say, "and more to the left."

Sitting this close to her, I could see all the tiny lines in the old woman's face.

"You look grand," she said. She looked at her daughter. "Ten years off," she said. "An absolute ten years."

Claire Anne looked nervous. "Cissie looked great before," Claire Anne said. "We all said that."

"She might have looked great before," Claire Anne's mother said, "but now she looks great and *younger*."

That alert old woman questioned me about everything, the local anesthetic, the swelling.

"Rhinoplasty," she repeated with pleasure. "Blepharophryplasty." She liked the words. She kept asking for more explanations.

"It makes me ill," Claire Anne said. "Stop! I won't be able to eat."

"Blood and guts," her mother said.

We were in my new apartment with the narrow ugly L-shaped living room. I'd brought all my old furniture. There seemed to be a place for everything.

"I'm opening another bottle," Bernadette said.

We were drinking the champagne that Imelda had brought, and in front of us on the coffee table was a tray of assorted cold cuts.

"I'll go now," Claire Anne's mother said. "Leave you girls to chitchat. I only dropped by for the unveiling."

"Good-bye, Mother," Claire Anne said.

"God," she said when the door had closed, "I bet my mother will do it too. Lift her face."

"Why not?" I said. "I did it."

"You look truly different today," Imelda said, "better than last week."

"It was the woman the doctor employs—the cosmetologist. I went to her this morning for the after-the-operation lesson—makeup, colors, hair redo."

"It certainly works," Claire Anne said. "Wait until your girls see you."

"Audrey was here yesterday," I said. "I think it upsets her. Fine, she kept saying. Real great. Eleanor hasn't seen me, of course. Maybe I'll fly out there—maybe."

We drank more champagne.

We got silly, we sat in that half-dark apartment and played games. Not games with boards or rules, we played nonsense games. Question games. Who was your most satisfying lover? What do you worry about most? What was the most selfish thing you ever did?

People I Knew
Now Residing in Florida

~~~~~~~~~

Schiffman sat next to me at the bar. Anywhere else it would have seemed early to be drinking. It didn't seem too early in Miami. Schiffman raised his glass. "Here's to you," he said. "Mucho congratulations."

"It doesn't really mean anything," I said. "It's only a trade fair."

Schiffman shook his head. "Come on," he said. "A blue ribbon is a blue ribbon. And you're tickled, admit it."

I smiled. "All right," I said. "Pleased, yes, pleased. They never awarded me anything before."

"Me," Schiffman laughed, "I'll never get anything—I know what I am—*vin ordinaire*, that's what—a *podler*. When rhinestones are in, I do rhinestones, when it's folk art, I give them folk art. You—you buck the tide—and with success."

"I sell," I said. "I'm all right. But then so are you. But let's not pretend—it's a trade—we're not artists."

"That I always believed," Schiffman said. "We are businessmen—*commercial* jewelry—the costume skills."

"Right," I said. Inside my pocket was the little plastic case, the blue ribbon. It was for my necklace. Everything this year was plain, everything was pseudo-Danish. My necklace was a thing of Roman scrolls, miniature cherubs, spirals. I loved it.

I looked at my watch. "Listen," I said. "It's only four-thirty. After we finish our drinks—want to take a walk?"

"A walk?" Schiffman put his hand on his heart. "More fearsome words were never spoken. I think I dreamt last night that someone would ask me to go for a walk. Yes, I think so. And you know what will happen, Sylvester?"

I shook my head.

"On the corner of Collins Avenue and Lincoln Road—I'll meet her. Exiting from Wolfie's, bagel bag in hand, she'll be there. You know who? My mother, Mama mine, Mammala—that's who."

"So your mother doesn't know you've come to Miami?"

"Know?" Schiffman laughed. "Sylvester, she doesn't know and furthermore she wouldn't care. Bagel bag? She'd be carrying books, this former librarian who has read the world's hundred best books *twice*. You got a mother?"

"Dead."

"My mother hates my guts, Sylvester. That was our last conversation. You're no son of mine, she said."

The bar was dark and too cold. I could see slivers of sunlight whenever the compressors turned on and the blinds on the windows blew outward. I wanted a walk.

"Listen, if you see her, you look the other way and she looks the other way and I'll make certain you don't trip as we pass her. Anyway, we could walk elsewhere—we could go down to Calle Ocho. Look at Cubans," I said.

Schiffman signaled the bartender. "Two," he said. "Don't protest—I'm paying. She hates me, Sylvester. Just because I told her she was to blame, it was her fault about my son Edward."

The glass in front of me was refilled, I sighed. "What did she do to your son?"

"To him personally nothing, but it's how she raised me. Super cautious, super involved. Therefore, I wouldn't let my kid alone. The psychiatrist said that was it. That's why Edward became a terrorist."

Two men looked at us. "Hush," I said to Schiffman. "Lower your voice."

"It doesn't matter now," Schiffman said. "We're talking fifteen years ago. A terrorist—my kid. You never saw him?"

"I only met you yesterday," I said.

Schiffman tapped his glass. "That's right, I remember. My boy was a jock, an athlete, a brunette All-American type. I believed he didn't have a thought in his head. Then suddenly he's blowing up buildings. A State University graduate—ended up where? In prison. A Schiffman first, let me tell you. And if I had been raised right, then this would never have happened."

"Maybe," I said.

"You got kids?"

"One daughter, she's married, lives in California."

"California?—that's where they keep Edward. Your mother raised you right, though, so your kid turned out okay."

"True," I said.

"You understand why I won't go with you?"

"I understand."

*   *   *

The sun was warm, a white light on everything. Why did they keep the insides of buildings so cold? These were tourist streets. Every restaurant had a sign offering *Early Bird Specials*. I patted my pocket, the plastic case. They had announced the award just a few hours ago. Who should I call? I'd call Joyce. She'd be genuinely pleased. It is only what you deserve, she'd say. Then I could call Cissie. Sylvester! Yes, she'd shout. Hooray for you, Brother!

I smiled and a street hawker of tours misinterpreted. "A cruise," he promised, stepping quickly to my side, receipt book in hand. "You won't be sorry, moonlight, lovely ladies. A bargain."

I moved on. "No speak English," I said.

"Español?"

"Rumanian."

Who else could I call? I had taken care of my former wife and my sister. My daughter wouldn't care. How nice, Daddy, she'd say. There were two women. I could telephone Charlotte. No, bad idea. I hadn't seen her in at least a month. Rachel? I could give her a call.

"I must ask you something." The man, dressed like a faded movie lover with an ascot tied around his neck, touched my arm.

Was I smiling again? I stepped away from the hand. "So long," I said.

"Sylvester?"

I stopped. Schiffman's mother in drag? I knew no one here. Not me. I stared at the old man—at an unfamiliar liver-spotted face.

"You look," the man said, "like an older version of yourself. Good thing you don't have a mustache or a beard, I never would have known you then. But you are the *same*. Sylvester?"

"Yes," I said.

"I'm Bill Spacedon, William Spacedon. Remember me? Athena's brother."

"Of course," I said, and held out my hand. I didn't recognize him, but I knew who he was.

"Don't tell me you live here now?"

"No," I said, "I'm in town for a meeting—a convention."

"You can't walk down these streets," the old man said, "without meeting someone you know. That's what I always say—and we've been down here five years."

I cleared my throat. "How is everyone? Your wife? And Athena?"

William shook his head. "Athena died five, six years ago. Heart attack, fast, the way to go. My wife—Kyle is in a nursing home—falling apart, poor old girl. But the rest of us are alive and kicking. Donna, Clement, and me—we share a condo in Sweetwater."

This wasn't a case of guess what happened to those we knew. Yet I stood there smiling, quite as if all the news were good. I wanted to pump the old man's hand and walk away. Athena was his sister. It wasn't as if I ever still *thought* about her—I couldn't pretend instant sorrow. But I was once going to marry Athena—so long ago that it was like thinking about something that could never have happened to you. Athena—if she were alive—would be an old woman. An older woman.

"Ever get back home?" William asked.

"No," I said, "I live in New York now—have for many years."

"I know what," William said, firmly holding my hand. "You are going to come to dinner."

"What?"

"Eating," William said. "At our table is the best food

around. Donna and Clement will be furious if I let you get away."

"I really can't," I said.

"Yes, you can," William said. He took out a notebook, a slim silver pen. "This is the address—take a cab—rent a car. I'm going to call Donna and tell her you're coming. Come at six-thirty."

It clearly didn't matter whether I said yes or no. William was determined. Had he always been stubborn? Yes, I remembered that. I took the piece of paper, it was pushed at me. All I had to do was not show up. The last time I saw any of these people I had been a boy, I had been twenty. The Spacedons—imagine running into them. I could see them—Donna, Clement, and William—sitting patiently and waiting for their guest. Waiting for me.

But what did I have to do that was better? Make whoopee with strangers? I walked back to the hotel. There was a message in my box. It was from Schiffman. *Let's eat dinner together,* he wrote. *There's a swell Polynesian place in the hotel or a jazz club with steaks. We don't have to hit the sidewalks at all.*

I arranged to rent a car. I called Schiffman. "Sorry," I said. "I've met some friends. I'm going to Sweetwater for dinner."

"Sweetwater?" he said. "I think my mother lives in Sweetwater."

I hung up.

The girl at the Avis desk took a map and a yellow pen and outlined my route. Easy, she said soothingly. And it was. I bought a box of candy and, in an impulse of excessive care, a bouquet of flowers, yellow and orange and white.

The Spacedons lived in a high-rise condominium, a skinny pale yellow building dotted with terraces, each with a brightly colored panel of plastic concealing its occupants. Ever since I ran into William I had looked at my reflection—in the hotel lobby, in the bathroom mirror. I looked like myself—I was recognizable. I rather liked that—to have grown up as expected.

The Spacedons lived on the twelfth floor. I sniffed the air. It was because of my sister. It was one of Cissie's peculiarities. Old people, she had declared, the air around old people is strange. I don't mean they don't bathe or that they wear stale clothes. It's not that—but there is an odor, a scent. Putrefaction, I said, and laughed at her. Early death, she had declared, the smell of cells dying. They don't smell, I said. Do so, she said.

When I knew the Spacedons they lived together in the same house—the mother, two sons, two daughters. I spent a lot of time in that house even though I was a kid and they were all older. The children were adopted—Donna, Clement, William, and Athena. Donna and Clement were married to each other, that was a tale, but they weren't blood kin. Actually, I think it turned out that Donna had never been legally adopted. The memory that embarrassed me was of Athena. Thinking of Athena. Had I been crazy? A twenty-year-old kid getting engaged to a thirty-six-year-old woman? Nuts, totally nuts.

But the Spacedons had been special to me. I remembered them sometimes better than my own family.

It was Donna who opened the door. "Sylvester!" She embraced me. I felt all right. She was not a disappointment, a slim tanned woman. A fashionable old woman with trimmed grey hair. "It's absolutely great to see you," she said and pulled me into the apartment. I gave her the flowers and candy.

When I thought about the Spacedons, they were of course unchangeable. I thought of them living in that house in a place of winters. The house filled with old furniture—all dark, all carved. Now behind Donna was a room totally pale and modern.

William beamed. "See," he said, "I knew he'd come."

I smiled back. I had been right about him—William looked like the neighborhood lover. Hadn't that been his reputation? Or perhaps I was thinking of some-one else.

Donna squeezed my hand. "Clement is out on the terrace," she said. "But before you see him—he's had a stroke, Sylvester. Oh he's all right, but he speaks a bit slowly."

I nodded. She guided me to the sliding glass doors. Clement sat outside in a yellow vinyl-covered chair. He looked old, frail. He had been the kind one, a decent man. Hard to believe that he was years younger than William, now bouncing about.

"Sylvester," Clement said carefully and clasped my hand with cool fingers. "Welcome back."

We talked throughout dinner. They were old friends, I was in the presence of old friends. There were flowers decorating the salad bowl and fresh salmon on a platter. I told the Spacedons about my award. They toasted my success. It was as though I were a boy again and eating with the family as I often had. I had loved this family. We spoke of Mrs. Spacedon, long dead. We talked about

William's wife, poor Kyle. You wouldn't know her, William said, a great bloated body. They told me about Athena. She had such a devoted husband, the musician from Baltimore.

"I'm glad she married. I was a foolish kid," I said.

"We forgave you long ago," Donna said.

"Yes," Clement said and nodded. "You were a young boy. A boy must be allowed to make his mistakes."

I thought there was an affectless quality to his voice. It must have been the stroke.

After dinner Donna gave me a tour of the apartment. All the rooms were bright and cheery. There was a bedroom for William and one for Donna and Clement. Then we had coffee and small pecan tarts out on the terrace. I told my old friends about my life, about my former wife, about my daughter in California.

"I'm thinking of getting married again," I said.

Donna clapped her hands. "Wonderful," she said. "You shouldn't be alone. Who is she?"

"Charlotte," I said. "Her name is Charlotte. She's a buyer in a department store. A very nice person."

"I'm sure," Donna said.

Donna went into the kitchen and William poured me a brandy. Clement had returned to the terrace, we could see his profile, motionless as he stared outward.

"Old times," William said. "It was fun. Although myself, I'm not much on reminiscing. It's the end when you do too much of that, you know."

"Yes," I said.

"But," he laughed, "it was fun. Brought back old times. Quite a life we had back then—living in the old house."

"I remember," I said.

William giggled. "You? You weren't part of it. Let me tell you, it was high jinks all right. Athena ever spill any of that to you?"

"What?"

"Hanky-panky," William said. "Lovebirds the four of us, and Mama Spacedon sitting downstairs scatty as an owl while the floorboards squeaked and the bed springs rumbled."

I left early, they were after all old, they seemed tired.

"Call us," William said, "next time you hit the Southern climes."

"Sure," I said.

Donna insisted on riding down in the elevator with me and walking to my car, which was parked in *Guests Only*. The night was hot, and the air held the smell of insecticide dripping from the palms and the crotons and the rich red hibiscus that surrounded the building. I unlocked the door to my car.

Donna put her hand on my arm. "It was really wonderful having you here," she said. "It would have pleased Mama so much. She was very fond of you."

"Yes," I said.

"And Sylvester," she said. "If William spoke to you—one mustn't believe too much of what William says. William is an old man."

I nodded and kissed her cheek. She stood there waving as I drove away. Orphans, I thought, they had all been orphans.

I followed the map, reversing everything, I got lost once. It was ten-thirty when I arrived back at the hotel.

You could shiver in that lobby. I had the hotel telephone operator connect me with Schiffman's room. "By accident," I said, "I ran into your mother tonight. And Schiffman—she forgives you."

Bad Girl

~~~~~~~~~~~~~~

Confessions
of a Bad Girl

~~~~~~~~~~~~~~~

My grandmother was born near the village of Nowogródek in Poland, also the birthplace of the poet Mickiewicz. My mother was born in Minneapolis, I think. I know absolutely where I was born, because the proof is staring me in the face. A certificate duly registered with the Bureau of Vital Statistics, Department of Health. Doctor's name Miller. Legitimate checked yes. City, Milwaukee. There was a mill and by the mill there was a walk and on the walk there was a key. I fingered the birth certificate, surprised to find it in the left-hand desk drawer. Why wasn't it in the safe deposit box next to the records of my husband and my daughters? I pushed the paper aside. I can't distract myself from my task. For three days I have been hunting for a misplaced checkbook. On the second day my husband said to me in disgust, "What is it this time? What have you lost?" I shook my head, I denied it. Nothing, I swore. Did he believe me? I immediately became secretive about the search, waiting until I was alone before digging under piles of papers, shuffling through miscellany in drawers, examining the contents of closet shelves. When my children were home there was always the thought that they had appropriated the lost item. How often had I replaced a lipstick or purchased a slip certain that one of my daughters had it, and then days later the shiny case that held Revlon's color of the month or the nylon slip with ecru lace would reappear, tucked away among my possessions. But the checkbook—this particular checkbook was large. My husband chose the style. We had a businesslike book, three checks across, three down. The dark brown vinyl cover was embossed by machine to look like alligator. And I couldn't find it. Suppose I admitted that I had lost the checkbook? But how could I admit that *I* had lost the checkbook. I wrote all the checks, kept the household accounts. I had been given as a present a small calculator, but even before its appearance, I had managed, my addition and subtraction were excellent.

Is the ability to lose papers determined at conception?— do zygotes when dividing carelessly drop those cells with the ability to keep everything on tap, in place. Where is it? my mother would say. We didn't know, none of us knew. Never leave anything behind, my mother said. Take everything, every crumb, sweep clean. Losers weepers, she would say, finders keepers.

I think that when I die someone will uncover my love letters and pity me. Couldn't she hold him? They will laugh at my lists. *This*, they will say, she saved. *This* bears witness. The answer to these sweet leavings?—False. These papers were not saved or pressed or treasured—they were eaten up by warrens of drawers, stuffed beneath beds, trapped between the covers of books.

Surely, then, the checkbook is somewhere. But when could I look? I had to limit the times of my search to one hour in the morning before I left for work, while my husband showered and dressed, and in the evening, during those moments when he was not aware of my purposes. And all the time, I had to conduct my affairs, pretend that this loss did not weigh upon my thoughts, and ordinary life always interrupted.

Suddenly I found my birth certificate again. This time in the closet among a pile of wrinkled receipts, appliance warranties, fat brown envelopes. I remembered having some papers in my hand, I remembered hearing my husband turn off the water in the shower. In haste I must have opened that closet door and dropped the papers on the shelf. If the same paper can turn up again—why not the checkbook? One shuffled in a circle through papers like an orphan child lost in the woods. See the tree, the branches a safety net of shade. Turn left, turn right—then there it is again. The tree.

My mother had papers too—string-tied packages of political pamphlets, the paper crisping at the edges, and receipts and clippings and notes that begged her to come at once or at the very least to send money. We carried all this with us when we moved. We carried it into the flat on Fon Nur Avenue where we lived for two years.

I paid attention to those papers. I was always sneaking around, looking through holes, hoping to see what was unspeakable, undone buttons, secrets written out. One of the first words I ever looked up was *anomie*. Did I ever run out of material? No. What I found at one age, I could rediscover later and uncover new meanings. There were certain funny things everywhere. For instance, my mother's parents disowned her—the word was *verleugnen*. The handwriting was heavily slanted, maybe a letter switched, a conjugation misinterpreted, but by and large, the consensus of my translaters was that the meaning was disowned. I read my mother's letters.

Sometimes friends moved, and letters came back marked address unknown. I'd read these too. Some I forgot about, others I used. In my play entitled "Robin's Home Again" I put in the contents of an entire letter. I altered names just the way I'd seen it done. The names have been changed to protect the innocent. This I printed on the bottom of page one.

On Fon Nur Avenue we once lived above a store. It was a liquor store, it was not dangerous. Every married woman in that neighborhood was fat. The only exceptions were Theresa's mother whose husband drank and two other women whose insides were said to be consuming them. All the rest were fat. Even my mother, although she was always talcumed and tightly corseted to fit into the white uniform that she wore to pretend to be a doctor's assistant. Just do what I say, he told her. If they call you nurse, don't contradict. The jobs I've held, my mother would say and sigh. But a working girl can always make her way.

I didn't plan to be fat or wear black crepe in winter and wallpaper prints in summer and puff upstairs with legs wrapped in Ace bandages. I didn't plan to be married. I planned to write plays.

For "Robin's Home Again," I needed costumes. If you're careful, my mother said, you can use the stuff in the boxes. There were three boxes of dresses set aside by my mother, clothes from a different time, she said. For me I selected a dress of dove-grey silk. I had at that time only one friend. It wasn't easy to pick something for Bridgy. Already at age ten her figure was inclined to marriage, and she got cranky if the dress chosen didn't immediately fit. Sometimes she would turn right around and go home. So I hunted through the box. For her I finally selected a loose chemise with a collar lined with sequins. Bridgy liked a touch of glitter.

The play was a romance, but there were no parts for boys. I knew no boys. It was just me and Bridgy. We would talk about lovers who would themselves never appear in the play. Most of my plays had just two characters.

In front of the mirror in my mother's bedroom, I tried a few of the lines I'd written. I'll cut you dead, I said. I'll never speak to you again. I repeated the lines, my voice grown distant and scornful, my reflection dove grey, my face white. Someday I would do that to Bridgy. I knew that even though it made me shiver to think about it. But yes, some day I would pass her on the street—plump, cranky, grown-up Bridgy—and I would cut her dead.

We did the play that afternoon, me in dove grey and Bridgy in salmon pink. It was a one-act play presented in the upstairs back hall. In my first version I found a letter and was to wonder whether or not to show it to Meg, the character played by Bridgy. If I gave that note to Meg, what would she say? *My God!* I thought she would say. *My God!* Would I be asked to keep a secret? One of my characters says that she never means exactly what she says. That was one of Bridgy's lines. I knew that she wouldn't say it right. No, Bridgy would make the words sound sour, like some line in a squabble. Imagine, Meg should say lightly, this old paper, a joke, part of a silly game—forget

it. For the performance I changed this part, did the letter
as dialogue.

ME: I was married once before—don't you know?—
         a long time ago.
BRIDGY: No, I never heard about that.

ME: Who did? A Mr. M. K. Gale—a saloonkeeper,
         a gambler, a dynamite man.
BRIDGY: You never spoke about him.

ME: Because it's done with, Meg, it's done with.
         No missus in front of my name anymore. No
         more Mrs. M. K. Gale. Forget whatever you've
         read about him. I'll tell you all next time we
         meet.

My mother left the kitchen and came into the hall.
"What's that?" she said.
"The play is over," I said.

That original letter had been written to Dot. I knew who
Dot was. Dot and my mother graduated from Blewett High
School. Dot came every couple of years all the way from
Evanston, Illinois, to spend a week with us. She had married
a man who owned a dry cleaning store, and she had three
boys. She showed photographs of them, great hulking boys.
I hoped never to meet them. Dot was a great visitor. I'm
here to pep up things, she'd say. Then for days she and
my mother would giggle, act silly, wear fancy bathrobes,
and buy liquor and mixes and pour drinks with names
like Whiskey Sour or Brandy Alexander. Dot would let
me sip from her glass and my mother would laugh and

say, Stop corrupting the child. Dot always had a sore on the corner of her lower lip that she tried to conceal with lipstick, but it was there, a silvery glow, a moist patch. I would never let Dot kiss me.

What did I overhear? Not everything, only bits, only the flavor of life. And his hand, Dot said, crept, yes crept, right up my leg under the dress to the garters. Midday, she said. A matinee.

I went into the bathroom and closed the door and sat on the edge of the tub so that my hand could creep up the side of my leg—up, up to where a garter might have been. Nothing to feel, though—just my thin, boney leg. Dot's garters hung from thin loops firmly sewn to the edges of her girdle. The dry, rubbery garters were bent and distorted where they had pressed into the richness of her flesh.

Some things remain lost forever. A creamy yellow blouse with a scalloped collar, the directions to a strange and complex game sent to my daughters from England by their father (the girls wept and accused me), the recipe for a sauce in which the exact proportions of the ingredients were needed to create a sharp mustardy flavor. I think I have its essence sometimes, but it was never right. Who is to say that what is lost is valuable? Only that what is lost is never forgotten.

I have dumped the contents of two drawers from the Empire highboy upon the floor. But the checkbook was not among those tumbled sweaters and scarves, notes, buttons, passports, and old gloves. "Cleaning?" my husband said to me suspiciously. "Sorting? Looking for something? What would you do if the IRS wanted to audit us? Tell me that?"

I left everything on the floor and went to call my daughter Eleanor and my daughter Audrey and invite them both to dinner on Friday night. It was close to the end of the month, and money was scarce—they both accepted.

The search must stop. I went to my office, where I was distracted, answered inappropriately, and was rude to my colleagues. I was firm in my position. I could get away with a certain amount of belligerence. "I want," I told my secretary, "the files on Hazelraft and on Kant and on McLowen." "All of that?" she said. "Yes," I ordered.

That evening my husband was late. I have a meeting, he said. I used the time to unfold the linen. The checkbook could be caught between the sheets. Before I finished, the telephone rang.

Aunt Arlette's daughter called me from St. Louis. Aunt Arlette has broken her leg. That's no small thing, the daughter says. For an eighty-year-old woman that can be the end. In her lobby, she continued, a good thing she wasn't alone. Send a card, she says. Take down the address. She names a hospital near Forest Park, near a wide boulevard. You must send a card. Yes, I say. Or else, the daughter warns, you have a heart of stone.

I will not send a card. It's not because I misplace the address of the hospital or because I forgot. I will not send a card, although I have a vision of the old woman slipping on a worn marble floor and sliding and rolling downward— why downward when the floor is level? Let the old woman sit up in her hospital bed with the pillows plumped around her and slit open her other envelopes. Hallmark has lost a customer in me.

*　　　　*　　　　*

In the hospital they stuck a needle in my arm with fluid that contained a radioisotope. A tag, they said. They could chart the course of that fluid by the presence of that tag.

Everything, I believe, has a tag. Find the tag and chart the course. You run your hand over a particular bit of blue cloth and the roughness on the tip of your finger rasping against the velvet makes you tremble. Your nostrils wrinkle at an unexpected scent and sniff the air. What's that? What's that? Tag.

I was in Aunt Arlette's apartment. She whispered in my father's ear. What's it to you? Why did you leave Springfield so suddenly? My father shook his head. He was her brother. My father was being sent somewhere to help a good union shop. At least that's what my mother said. Be a good girl, my mother said. See you in apple blossom time. Was I afraid? Did I feel abandoned? Count the days, my mother said, and marked important circles on a calendar.

For seven weeks I would stay with Aunt Arlette. And Aunt Arlette would say, This is my brother Joe's child. Yes, she's a big girl. I would nod and bob. But this was only to her friends. Landsleit were different. They rushed at me, no introductions needed. My father's relatives roamed through that apartment in startling numbers. I was from a family of four. We had always lived up North. Names were shoved at me. I was embraced by fierce ladies, buried in their soft flesh while brooches pricked my cheek. Who does she look like? they asked each other.

I had never seen Aunt Arlette before. But, she said, you have. When you were three, she said, and once as a baby. I ate breakfast and lunch in the kitchen with Aunt Arlette and a woman named Rae, who did the cleaning.

What happened? All that happened were the holidays. I

had never known so many holidays. And for the holidays the dining room doors were pushed back into the walls. Back and forth I would slide these doors of oak until I was warned. Then the dining room table was stretched outward with inserts of wood. White linen cloths, plates dazzling with painted red flowers entwined with large green leaves. Aunt Arlette would take off her black crepe dress and her gold bracelets and cover her black rayon slip with a long white apron like butchers wore and stand next to Rae in the kitchen and cook. The first course was already on the table when everyone arrived. On small clear glass plates were pale grey fish balls, two on each plate, balanced in a cup of lettuce leaves, the balls separated by a pink-toned scraping of horseradish. Never had I eaten such food, how I disgraced myself, gagging on the taste of that fish. The cousins my age, all alien, giggled. She's barfing, one said. My plate was removed. An excuse was made. She is not feeling well. Could this be said every time?

I learned which odors I could not bear, knew when the fish balls were being made. On the stove would be the simmering broth, afloat in the pot the skeletons of fish bobbing to the bubbling motion, fish heads, bits of onion. The smells of oceans blowing through the rooms. Winter carp, whitefish, pike.

Rae was sympathetic. Don't worry, she said. Gefilte fish is an acquired taste. Buck up, kid. Was it always a holiday? How often did God rest? It was a holiday. They set the table, ten places down one side, ten places down the other. The grey fish balls in front of each chair. Except for me. Suddenly for me there was a scoop of tuna fish salad cozily placed within its half-circle of lettuce. I didn't mind tuna fish salad. I could always eat tuna fish salad. There,

Aunt Arlette said coming up behind me. See what I've done.

They arrived, the people, and filled up the rooms. I was all right. I even laughed and spoke to those cousins. It was the first bite. The first forkful of tuna fish salad. There among the pink flakes, most cleverly disguised, were bits of mashed fish ball. I tasted that, held that in my mouth. There was noise at the table, there was much conversation. I left the table unnoticed. Went to the back of the apartment. Opened the bathroom door. I spit the hated mouthful into the toilet. Aunt Arlette came into the room, did not knock, pushed the door against the wall. She stood there staring at me, a firm woman in black crepe and gold bracelets, and she drummed her long fingernails against the tile wall. I thought so, she said. I thought so.

I paid our bills on the fifth of each month. The truth of it was that I did not always do this in the same manner. Sometimes I sat at my desk in the bedroom, but sometimes I wrote the checks in the morning while drinking my coffee. And still again I occasionally slipped the checkbook into my briefcase and wrote the checks at work. I could not imagine that checkbook lost. Someone's hands turning back the brown cover and tracing our lives from those stubs. What would they make of us? The purchases at the flower shop, the codes and initials, the rent, the habits of extravagance, our tendencies. I vowed that I would try again to remember what I had done. I concentrated while I made my morning cup of coffee. The brew was strong and as brown as the cover of the checkbook.

My husband came into the room. "This was probably it," he said. "Here you are—the object of all the hustle-bustle searching." He handed me a copy of Updike's *The*

Witches of Eastwick. "A fourteen-day library book," he said, "between the folds of the Sunday Travel Section about to be thrown down the chute. My arms were full of newspapers. The book suddenly fell out. And look at the fine! I bet you owe six dollars."

It is difficult to remove books from a library today unless they have been duly recorded. There are magnetic strips in books or something. Books must be defused before they can be removed. This is an innovation. I imagine that this must save libraries enormous sums of money. At one time I smuggled books from libraries. Yes, I did. Not with the intention of keeping them or otherwise harming them. But nevertheless I took them. In among the books properly credited to me I would on occasion secrete another book. I was then duly bound to read that book. The idea was Freddy's—oh not to take a book, but to alter my habits, to lift, he said, my limitations. You've read nothing, he accused. I couldn't believe that. I had spent endless hours reading books. Had I done much else? Whatever did they teach you on the prairies, Freddy said. He rattled off names—Cabell, Ford, Canfield, Rolland, Weatherwax, Norris. And no, I had not read them. See, he said.

How to make my choice of a book special? I mean how would I know whether or not I had deliberately picked that book, thus ensuring a continuation of my limited experience. Random choice. I decided to snatch my special books from a wooden cart where they were stacked to be reshelved. The books taken this way were not classifiable. I read masonry self-taught, I read a romance about a girl named Denise and a man named Jed who spirited her away to the Isle of Corfu, I read a history of Flemish painting, a book on meatless cooking, ten mysteries. I read one hundred and twelve books. I believe that my experience can be equated with the apochryphal story that if a chimpanzee types long enough he will re-create Shakespeare. Never once in my thefts did I encounter anything of Shakespeare's.

I hadn't returned the books. Meant to, but hadn't. They dispersed themselves in the corners of Freddy's apartment, fell into drawers in the kitchen, were trapped between magazines in the bedroom.

Be a doll, Freddy said. Oversee the move, will you. I've arranged everything with the movers, and my mother is expecting the load. Isn't it better to sell? I said. Instead of shipping everything to Ohio. Sell? Freddy said. This furniture cost a fortune. What isn't an antique is an original. Okay with me, I said. Freddy kissed my lips. Off to Spain, he said, and went to Kennedy. I had to get boxes, I had to defrost the refrigerator. I packed everything. I called Freddy's mother in Cincinnati. She was not happy to hear from me. Of course I have enough room to store everything, she said. Who are you to ask that?

What did I have in Freddy's apartment? Only my clothes and a reading lamp. And, of course, one hundred and twelve library books. Cleaning that apartment had not been easy. I rewarded myself with the mattress to the double bed, one grey chair with lion's claws that gripped the floor, and all the drapes, which strangely fit the windows in my new apartment. I could have packed the books, except that packing them seemed to make them permanently mine. I could not do that. I stacked them in paper shopping bags, averaging ten to twelve books per bag. Should I take them back where they belonged? Was that dangerous? The books actually came from four different libraries. I borrowed a car from a girl named Sharon who actually liked to lend it. Drive with care, she said, but have a good time. I packed the trunk of the car with the books. At nine p.m. I left the city and drove up the Saw Mill Parkway. A library is a library after all. I had a map and a county telephone book for addresses. I was looking for libraries with night depositories. If seen, I had stories ready. The neighbors, I would say, left me their books to return before they moved away. The children, I would say, off to camp. The first library was a colonial brick and the night depository, a grey metal mailbox apparatus. *Return Books Here.* Three bags filled it. I saw no loiterers, but I trembled. Two more stops and the books were gone, tumbled into those chutes, a grab bag of words. I drove back to the city, paused beneath the abandoned West Side Highway, and flung the empty shopping bags into the Hudson.

Dot used to send Christmas cards, a five-dollar bill enclosed in each. Those I found in the desk, sent to me while I was in high school, have her old address in Illinois. After I went away to college, she stopped.

They still had sororities at the state university when I was there. The closest I came to that kind of camaraderie was when I shared a house on Market Street with three other girls. It was an ugly house, drafty and with a fearsome attic from which we regularly heard scraping noises. Mrs. Rochester, we decided. It's her, we'd shout.

Get 'em, old girl! But we never went upstairs to investigate. In fact, we did nothing to that house—no coats of paint, no posters on the wall, and at the end of the year we all moved out.

I was living in that house when my mother went to Florida for a month. Dot invited me, my mother said on the telephone. Dot's husband had died abruptly one morning. A coronary, my mother said. The way to go, one-two-three, she said. Dot owned a condominium in Sarasota. The boys? I asked. What happened to her boys? One is an insurance broker, my mother said, one has the store, and one is vice-president of a games factory.

An evening in March the three girls and I sat on the grime-smoothed chairs in the living room of that rented house. We drank beer, and I did Dot for those girls. The hand, I said, crept—yes, it did—it cre-ept up my leg heading straight for that garter. I mimed the actions. Oh God, one of the girls said, wiping her eyes, holding her sides.

Audrey and Eleanor were eating dinner. I had made roast chicken, and everyone sat at the table comfortably picking the last shreds from the bones. Both girls were wearing jeans and old blouses. They didn't look alike, Audrey was thin and almost elegant, Eleanor short and plump.

"I don't understand," my husband was saying, "why the two of you don't share an apartment. You could do with less room then. You're sisters. No strangers poking in your things."

"Why," Audrey said, "should a stranger poke in my things?—and why would I care?"

Audrey and Eleanor exchanged glances.

That evening after my daughters had returned to their own apartments I found the checkbook unexpectedly as I packed my briefcase for the morning. I must have brought the checkbook home from work in a large manila envelope. It looked all right, it seemed to be intact. For safety I put it inside my overnight case, locked the suitcase, and put it under the bed. I was content to know that inside that suitcase was the brown-covered checkbook.

My husband came into the room as I was undressing. "Not a bad evening," he said. "The girls were fairly decent for a change." He looked down at the floor. There was a paper on the floor. "What's this?" he said and bent over to pick it up. It was my birth certificate. "Doctor Miller," he read out loud. "Legitimate, yes." He laughed. "You really do need someone to take care of you." He embraced me, pulled me close, whispered my name. Did he know who he held in his arms? *Conspirator.* Finders keepers. *Thief.* Losers weepers. *Girl with heart of stone.*

Three Girls
on Holiday

～～～～～

This play is definitely too expensive to produce. I mean, first of all you have to have the Caribbean. I don't intend to have a cardboard sea horizon or a puddle of sand stage center, I want real water, real beads. The element in caps. THE ELEMENT. When Ralph says to his wife, "How would you say the water is? You are in it so much." And she (Donna) is going to reply, "The water is soft and holding and blue. The water is blue, blue, blue. The water is azure. There are small tidal movements. There are eddies in the current. There is salinity. Warmth and breezes in moderation." I want just that. I want the audience to feel the pull of that water. Can they keep themselves from vaulting in? I want arms to tremble slightly with chill. Turn down the air conditioning, someone in the audience should scream. We're wet, don't you see?

❋   ❋   ❋

Now, scene one and the curtain is up. Donna will be there. We'll show her preparing for the morning. She drapes around her neck eleven gold chains of varying lengths. From an eighteen-inch chain hangs a diamond-studded Star of David. From one of the longer chains there dangles a Chinese ideogram promising happiness. These chains form a bib in the neckline of her white caftan. Her skin must be carefully tanned. One of those tans that drives everybody crazy.

Donna looks in the mirror as she paints on coral lipstick with a narrow brush. On her eyelids she dabs green eyeshadow. Her short hair is the color of copper, too bright, too harsh. She knows that, but it pleases her anyway.

She is pleased with everything about herself, even though she knows she looks a sight. She has selected this sight, picked it herself. She slips on shoes and goes out. To meet Ralph.

They have been in the hotel for two days, and they will stay eight more. Summer is not the right season for this hotel. That's why Donna looks so different. If the season were winter, the hotel would be filled with women who looked just like Donna.

This trip is in celebration of a wedding anniversary. Pick any number you want.

Donna walks down the hall to the elevator, her backless white clogs snapping.

Enter girls.

Donna turns at the sound of keys. Three girls coming out of the gloom towards the elevator. They each wear jeans and tee shirts with smart sayings. Donna knows about girls who travel in threes, and she's right. One nice-looking, one so-so, and one an absolute disaster.

*   *   *

Donna hears the keys behind her in the elevator. She half-turns and sees the gesture one girl makes to her neck. They are looking at the chains. The elbows go out to exchange nudges. Donna stands motionless, so graceful.

Caribbean lobby. Olde leather couches, a wind machine for wind-cooled effect. Ralph puffing his cigar and waiting.

Ralph is masculine, tanned, hard-muscled from something. He is one of those I-am-what-I-am Ralphs. In his fifties, he is handsome and infatuated with Donna.

Donna and Ralph are in love. Old-fashioned love. Sexual love. An ardor that is steaming from them. The scene on their balcony. A cardboard moon would do here. They know how to excite each other. But no pornography. They would even be fully dressed. "Ramón," Donna will whisper, and Ralph will answer, "Donnatella."

The elevator reaches the lobby. Exit Donna. The wind machine turns, and Donna's caftan billows. She looks for Ralph. She sees him, waves, and he comes to join her. Together they go into the hotel restaurant for breakfast. Ralph has found a newspaper. The wrong city, he says. But English is English. Donna follows the waiter. She marches past the table where the three girls sit. She isn't accustomed to humor directed so openly at her.

She will put the girls away from her thoughts. If Ralph is having a good time, she'll have a good time.

Ralph has hinted at a surprise. Tonight, he has said. Donna has seen the blue velvet box hidden in his suitcase. Who cares what's inside? Blue velvet rarely disappoints. Ralph was always a good sport. She will do anything for him.

* * *

Flashback. Lower the lights. This is how Ralph met Donna. He came to the coastal Texas town where she lived one spring. We can't do the whole state of Texas. Yes, I realize that. We could play the scene like *Our Town* at this point. People. No scenery. *Suggestion.*

Obviously, Donna will have to do the meeting alone while standing under a dim spot to the left of the proscenium. Careful. We are not looking at the native girl meeting white man (gringo). Donna is a temptress. Do I really want to do their meeting in a soliloquy?

Donna will be talking about a small Texas coastal town. Loneliness. Dust. That's it. I'd like to paint dust. Like a wind machine directed at the audience sending fine red dust. No, I don't care if the color is not geographically correct. I want fine red dust blown out.

Ralph has come to town to work in his cousin's fruit business. Nothing needed here. A grape is a grape. Donna works in the office typing invoices. She loves Ralph so much, so totally, that her mother is frightened. "Forget it," her mother says. "It'll be nothing."

Was her mother right? Ralph left. He had to return home. He fought with his cousin. I can't take that, he said. All day orders—do this, do that. Understand, Donna?

Donna followed him. She must, she said. In Miami, Ralph was easy to find. He had not lied about anything. He had opened his own business now. He was burnt black from the sun.

He was glad to see her. This is not about if she hadn't come—because she did come. She was as attractive as he remembered. She had come just to find him. She wasn't pregnant. He had at that time a mother, a father, a married brother, and many other relatives.

The stage is dark. A dim spot on the table and two chairs. This is the scene with Donna and the rabbi. She has come to him for instruction. She wants to convert. The rabbi's name is Pearlman. He is only thirty. He is not interested. The conversion scene is good, especially the rabbi. Pearlman is young and devout. He does not want Donna's conversion. She sees that. They confront each other. Pearlman is firm and realistic, no mystic. She is the shiksa.

Back to the hotel and the island. The island is just a small, tight circle. Wherever Donna goes, the girls soon appear. Their whispers grow louder. They notice her brooches, her flowered blouses. One grows bolder and steps sharply in a doorway in front of Donna. "Oh pardon me," she says, blocking the way.

Donna has a brick wall put up around the garden behind the house in Miami. It cuts off part of the view. But she wants it, therefore she can have it. There is a gate at the back, and you can open the gate and go out to the dock and the water.

The scene with Ramón. This must be very complex. There has to be an entire street. No, we cannot do the fog and Spanish music bit. The street must be full of people. They must belong there. What a casting problem! Donna walks there with such ease. The swaying of her body is not exaggerated. She is with Ralph. "Ah Ramón," she calls. "See how the women look at you. See the envy. My

Ramón, my pequeño." Ralph laughs and accepts. The love names of the honeymoon. Dark-skinned, dark hair. "My Ramón," she whispers. Donna is happy. The music is from a distance. A beat though, a distinctive beat. When Ralph and Donna move, it must be in time to the music.

Set the next act in the casino. Donna gambles in the casino without any real interest. Win or lose, her expression does not change. The pit bosses watch her. Gangster types. They are front and center, and Donna obligingly fades into the dark background. The girls are at the slot machines. They cannot play long. They pay no attention to Donna. They are praying. One bunch of quarters and I will be very good. One win, one flashing bell, and someone will notice.

One day sitting on a lounge chair in the sun Donna writes a postcard to Naomi. Naomi is the child who once went away. How shall I show Naomi? Do I want to destroy prescience, stultify imagination? Young Naomi in terror. Naomi alone. Not true. Naomi tough as nails. Young Naomi enjoying freedom from obligations. Young Naomi having a ball. Naomi going bye-bye.

Ralph could afford detectives. They searched for Naomi, but they didn't find her. She's dead, Ralph swore. She's dead. Donna knew that wasn't so. Naomi could take care of herself. Naomi had once turned to Donna and said, "I hate you." "It doesn't matter," Donna had replied. "I will still be your mother." "Fool!" Naomi screeched another time. Donna left her and went into the garden.

How had they found Naomi? She sent a letter. It was on white paper, the kind you buy in drugstores in celluloid boxes labeled *Stationery of Distinction*. I am all right, Naomi wrote. I live here now. I have a husband. His name is Parel. Ralph wept, clutched the letter, and laid his head on Donna's lap. Baby, he sobbed. Baby.

How far do the girls go? Hell, they're puppies who have found their bone. Only instead of eating it all at once, they'll kick it around. You know that if anything more interesting came up, they'd vanish.

Donna is in a store where she is buying a bracelet for Naomi. She selects it with care. Even though Naomi will not wear it. Naomi will never wear it. When she looks up, the ends of the silk scarf that is knotted around her throat fall across the counter. The girls are standing outside the store staring through the window. Their eyes are wide in identically simulated expressions of wonder.

Once Donna and Ralph had gone to Maine where Naomi lived in a small house with Parel. They made pottery there. Parel had studied art. He had always intended to become a potter, he said. Naomi had a little boy. No, I want Naomi's boy there. That neurasthenic child. A bland bowl of porridge. Naomi's husband is polite. Parel is decent and upright. The whole pottery shed must be there, clay, wheels, sawdust.

Every holiday Naomi and Parel send gifts. They never forget. Large wooden crates arrive, and deep in the cushion of shredded paper are the gifts. A vase. The card says that it is called Star of Night. A large bowl called Harmony. A plate called Silence. The glaze is blue into green. The vase Donna puts on the wide windowsill in the den.

The plate and bowl she puts in the china cabinet. Whenever there are too many pieces of pottery, Donna takes the oldest and throws them away. It never bothers her. They are all alike.

On the postcard that Donna is writing from the island, she thanks Naomi for the plate called Celebration.

One day Ralph wants to see a man about a deal. Donna does not say not now. She never says words like that, or don't leave me alone. Go, she whispers and kisses him. Me, I'll lie in the sun or swim.

The girls are on the beach, as she knew they would be. Two in bikinis, the heavy one in a black one-piece suit. Their suntans imperfect, half burn. Donna selects a lounge chair. The beach is small. Behind her dark sunglasses she sees that they have spotted her. Today Donna wears the flowered suit, the one bought in Hawaii. It is cut low in the front with peekaboo lacing that is more provocative than a bikini. It is a favorite suit. Donna closes her eyes. She has brought no book. She has brought nothing with her but her bathing cap. Would they last the afternoon? But what else could they do? What else waited for them?

Two of them pass her on their way to the refreshment booth. "I do like colors," one says. "Red and blue and yellow." "Don't forget purple," the other replies.

Donna does not open her eyes. The large flowers on the suit are yellow. The centers are blue. The leaves are red. The background is midnight purple.

At three o'clock Donna stands up. She tucks her hair into the red rubber cap slowly, pushing each strand high. She walks across the sand to the stone steps that lead to the small bridge. Beyond the bridge is the water unprotected by the little net that guards the beach. The blue water is there.

Donna is on the bridge. She dives into the water, hitting it cleanly and going deep before she surfaces. The water is warm and soothing. A calm, quiet sea. Donna begins a crawl. She is relaxed, pushing her way through the water. She hears the splashes behind her and the laughter. They have dived into the water. The three girls swim behind her in a straight line, keeping their distance, perhaps thirty or forty yards.

Smell the water now? Feel its invitation? Donna concentrates on the blue. The sun makes circles in the water. Blue on the outside and green on the inner. Her arms cut from blue to green. There is no grace to her movements. It is very different from the way she dances. She splashes too much. Her arms seem to make sharp angles. Not like the girls slipping through the water. See their arms and legs move? One, two, together.

Donna senses that the girls raise their heads and smile at each other from time to time as, spread out like a fan, they pace her. How good her body feels. She is not stressed. Her movements are almost lazy. Donna shifts into a butterfly breast stroke, pulling herself through the water. Behind her now the fan moves faster too, and almost on signal they pass her as her arms splash awkwardly. To a syncopated beat the arms of the girls rise and fall with elegance. The seabirds will observe, Donna knows. She goes back to a crawl. On cue the girls go slower, and she is allowed to pass them. Can she hear them laugh in the water? Donna wonders. Her body floats buoyantly on the waves. Movement, movement. Crawl, crawl.

The fan catches up. The fan passes her. The fan drops back. Donna goes faster. Had they noticed her arms before? Had they noticed the muscles? No, her arms are smooth. Like theirs. Donna goes faster. The fan is catching up. Then Donna goes faster. She goes through circles. Dark blue, light blue, green. Now there is horizon. She slows, and the fan approaches. At the moment when they think they have reached her, she pulls away. Quickly, the fan struggles forward. Donna is pushing away the water. It holds her up nicely. Swim, little girls. Huff and puff goes the black swimsuit. The horizon spreads front and back. Darkness.

Golden spot on stage right. Shadowy figure who represents Donna selects a dress to wear from a pile of garments on a chair. She holds the dress up against her body. The sound of music with a strong rhythmical beat is heard. Donna sways her hips. Ah, Ramón, she whispers. She moves her arms as if she were cutting through water. Two couples dance past her. Light dims. Music fades.

The entire stage is now lit. Donna turns in a wide half circle towards the shore. She is a red ball bobbing on the surface.

She will appear on the stage for the curtain calls and the standing ovation, still in her suit with the water glistening on her body. The three girls will stand on the far left with seaweed clinging to them, their skin already faintly blue.

Still, if the out-of-town audience disapproves, we'll reverse the final scene. We can even make the change during intermission. There's nothing absolute in these affairs.

Challenge

~~~~~~~

To the left of the desk, a large regulation teak veneer desk for Management Classification M-1, along the short wall, stood the credenza balanced on its stubby stainless steel legs. The floor was covered with industrial grey carpet, low loop pile. She had pushed her chair back from the desk, leaned back in that pushed chair, and thinking and staring she saw the paper beneath the credenza. The distance from bottom of credenza to floor was only five inches, and she bent over, breasts resting in her lap, for a better view of the paper. The paper was approximately fourteen inches back from the front of the credenza, the credenza itself was thirty-six inches deep. How long had the paper been there? She looked at her desk. On the far left-hand corner was her In Box. She tried to visualize a breeze strong enough to lift a paper and send it floating downward beneath the credenza. Alternatively, someone carrying a paper to her, dropping it, and being distracted as it floated downward. But that would be downward. Then someone leaving the office had kicked or otherwise moved the paper. And the paper had landed then beneath the credenza. The paper appeared to be standard typing size, eight and one-half inches by eleven. She bent further, dropping her head between her legs, and turning her neck. The printing was indistinct, she thought she detected the blue markings at the top of the standard company memo, the logo design. She raised her head, rushing blood made her dizzy, painful ringing in her ears.

What could be missing? Had her tickler file been ignored?

She pushed the Intercom button on her telephone for her secretary.

Madeleine answered. "Yes?"

"Have I signed everything?" the woman asked. "All recent correspondence, memos and everything?"

"Yes—everything," Madeleine said.

The woman disconnected. Would the secretary remember? Even more, would the secretary care? Was a letter or memo missing? If she had failed to answer it, how much was jeopardized? She picked up her cup of coffee. The brew was slightly chilled. The coffee was in a china cup, patterned with blue flowers, a vitreous shining cup. She washed that cup herself every day. She sometimes saw cups that other people were given to wash. These cups were often placed rim down on the edge of the washroom sink.

She looked at her appointment book, there were three more people due that morning. She didn't wish to see any of them. She pushed her chair closer to the desk. Before, she hadn't seen the paper when her chair was properly positioned near the desk, but now she saw it. She saw it if she turned her head even slightly to the left, her eyes converged on it.

She picked up the telephone receiver and pressed Intercom. "Madeleine," she said. "Come in."

Madeleine entered carrying the yellow legal-size pad on which she always made notes.

"Madeleine," the woman said, "I must be missing something."

"What?"

"Look," she said and pointed, "a paper is down there."

Madeleine looked down. Standing upright she could not see the paper. She bent over from the waist, she was plump, she wore a green wool dress that wrinkled at the waist. "I see the paper, some paper," Madeleine said.

"What is it?"

Madeleine hesitated. "I don't know," she said.

"Did you drop something?"

"No," Madeleine said, her voice sounded annoyed.

They waited. Madeleine put one hand on top of the credenza for balance and went down on her knees on the grey carpet. Her fleshy wrist would not edge easily beneath the bottom rim of the credenza. Abruptly, without pushing her arm very far beneath the credenza, she stood up, her cheeks flushed from the exertion. "I've torn my stockings," she said. "I could feel them rip when I bent. I don't know what that paper is, I can't reach it, but it's not mine."

Madeleine smoothed her dress, looked down at her leg where a band of nylon was parting, a ridge of white flesh oozing forth. She was angry. "Ripped," she said. "Is that all?"

The woman nodded.

The woman couldn't postpone her first appointment. It was with two assistant supervisors. The meeting set for ten-thirty. Someone knocked at her door, turned the knob. "Sorry," the man said, he was shorter than the man behind him. "But your secretary wasn't at her desk."

"All right," the woman said. "Come in."

The men knew that they should have been announced. Should they have waited? They exchanged glances.

"Sit down," she said.

The short man and the other one sat across from her. They had a report to discuss. She had read it. "I don't know," she said. "If the costs have been properly contained. I don't know."

They looked upset.

From where they sat, could they see the paper? The chairs were sharply angled into a conversational half circle.

"We worked a long time on the report," the shorter man said.

She wondered who else had seen the report. "Work more," she said. "Rebudget, recalculate."

The men stood up, they were dismissed.

She waited until they were gone. She walked around her desk and sat in one of the black leather chairs, the one that the short man had sat in. She inclined her body, crossed her legs. Hadn't he rested his elbow on the chair arm, tilted his head? She did the same. You could see one corner of the paper, see it as a white triangle on the greyness. She tried the other chair. If that man had moved forward—had he?—if so, then the white triangle grew larger. They *knew* then that there was a paper on the carpet beneath the credenza.

She walked back to her chair. She sat down and opened her middle drawer. She pulled out the Intra-Building Telephone Book, found the number. Never mind Madeleine. She dialed Housekeeping. "Send me a supervisor," she ordered.

They sent up a young black man wearing a blue suit

and carrying a clipboard with attached pencil. He was polite. "What's wrong?" he asked. He looked around the office.

"Do they vacuum under my credenza?" she said. "I don't believe that a vacuum can reach under that space, can it?"

"A hose," the man said. "They use a hose."

"How often?" she said. "No, don't bother to answer. There is dust under there, paper clips, bits of strange-colored fuzz, who knows what else."

"Ma'am?"

"Look for yourself."

The man bent over. "Yes," he said. "I'll have it taken care of."

She knew that he had seen the paper, he couldn't have missed the paper. "I would like that cleaned up now," she said.

"Well," he said, "I'll order the evening crew to move the credenza and do a proper job."

"Not satisfactory," she said. "I mean now. My company pays sufficient rent to the building management for proper maintenance."

"It will disrupt," the man said.

Two men wearing freshly ironed khaki pants and shirts entered the office. The men appeared to be too slight to move the credenza. The woman with them wore a khaki dress and a cloth cap that completely covered her hair. She pulled a tank vacuum with a long hose looped around her shoulders. The three employees spoke together, paying no attention to the woman sitting behind the desk. The two men pushed at the credenza. "Is it loaded?" one said.

"I have no attention of removing my files, if you mean that. Get more help!" said the woman behind the desk.

The men sighed and pushed harder, they strained and grunted. The credenza moved, it slid forward at an angle coming close to the edge of the desk. The carpet exposed by this move was pale and mottled. What was there? A few paper clips, rubber bands, a pencil, a ballpoint pen, tumbleweeds of dust. The piece of paper.

"What's that?" she said.

The men hesitated. One picked the paper up. She thought he was looking at it.

"Give it to me," she said and held out her hand.

"Take it easy, lady," the man said. "We're union."

But he gave her the paper.

She read the paper. It was not what she had expected. It would not have been missed. Nevertheless, someone must have put it there. Suppose another piece of paper appeared there. It could happen. If she had been alone, she would have wept.

Work Habits

~~~~~~

"I have succeeded," my father said. "So can you. I could tell you such glowing tales of my success. But I'll lay my cards on the table. Nothing is permanent."

My father sat me down. "It happened," he said, "when you were seven. Can you be expected to remember from when you were seven? Your brother was fifteen. What happened to him later I put right at their door—right at the door of the Empress Chocolate Company—'Sweetest Sweets in the Ozarks.' In March when the spring water ran the coolest, they pink-slipped me like a candy surprise. My life will henceforth go down unknown paths, I said to myself. Meanwhile, I had to go home. I was consolidating it all in my mind, the reorganizations, the red columns, the declining sales, the American sweet tooth gone cavity-free. To this I added the factors of my age, my wife, my not fully grown children.

"I came home. We had dinner. We had breaded veal chops, mashed potatoes, peas, salad. Your mother cleared the table, no one helped. She brought in the poached pears, the coffee. In the living room in a glass bowl were the Empress's finest chocolates—dark with hazelnuts. I had the whole event planned, net profits, gross losses, escrow accounts. But instead I sipped my coffee—black, unsweetened—and blurted it out. They let me go today, I said.

"Your brother looked at me. He had the hardness of city babies. Do we have for bread and so, or not? he says. Of course, I say. As I edged towards the door torn with pain, you all shrieked and tore at my clothes. Where are you going? you shouted."

My father kissed me, a kiss of luck. I went into success. Three jobs in fifteen years. I went from Chicago to Detroit to New York. I moved up, I moved into middle management. But I had hopes, dreams, thoughts of further promotions. "It'll come," my husband said. My husband was very loyal. "They'll recognize your worth."

Sometimes I wrote out a letter of resignation. But I didn't submit it. I stuffed it into my purse and took it home to burn.

My friend Arthur and I once collaborated on a booklet called "How to Stay Awake in Meetings Without Dancing"—it was rather funny. We duplicated it and passed it around at the office. It was much enjoyed and got us into no trouble. "You were lucky," my husband said.

"Does it bother me that I now have only a daughter for the future? Not at all," my father wrote. "Trust people. Once I got on a bus without any change. I stood there holding a dollar bill. Excuse me, I said. Does anyone have any change? My voice was low, apologetic. I was young, not yet assertive. No one moved, no hand slid forward. Listen, I said, I must stay on this bus. I'll be late for work.

I might lose my job. One set of hands moved slowly to purse, opening vinyl purse made to look like leather with pretend straw handles. From a woman, old, vain. Here is the change, she said. Bless you, I said."

I went to work every day. Middle management goes to work every day. In the genesis of the week, I came alive in time for Tuesdays. What happened on Tuesdays? On Tuesdays the section supervisors met at ten. We sat there, a dozen of us. They fed us coffee from a soup-scented urn and glazed doughnuts. One of the section supervisors did imitations. He did Clark Gable. He did Charles Boyer. He did Jerry Lewis. Sometimes district supervisor Barlow conducted our meetings. We heard from him a lot about feedback and interface. Arthur can't stand him.

"God, it's him today," Arthur whispered to me. "Want to interface for lunch? Feed your face instead of your back." I would have liked to hit him before I started to giggle. Whenever I said "Shut up," everyone heard, no matter how low my voice. So I stepped on Arthur's foot instead.

"Wait," Barlow said at the end of the meeting, his finger pointing at me.

Arthur made a face. "Zap time," he whispered.

They were homing in on my department. They were asking me to fire Dorothy.

"Today," Barlow said.

I nodded.

Actually, the firm discharged people quite regularly. How were they chosen? I had once asked Arthur. "A formula," he had said. "Productivity plus seniority times spit in the air—that's how."

Dorothy had the third office down the corridor from mine. She had been with the company for about a year. I looked over her personal data in my folder. She was one year younger than I. She was divorced, there was one child.

It was eleven-thirty when I returned to my office. Arthur had always advised, "Fire them after lunch. The full stomach makes them soporific." I never turned my back on advice. I stood at my door and looked down the corridor. No activity. All the doors were closed.

I waited until ten past one, and then I dialed Dorothy on the intercom. "Would you step into my office, please," I said. On my desk was an envelope with a check. We gave money instead of two weeks' notice. They didn't like anyone to hang around, a disturbance, people took sides.

Dorothy came in. I had invented a mythology about her. Her skirt was wrinkled. Dorothy did not care. She did not pull it tight when she sat down. I visualized her as ugly, preferably with warts. Two warts on the nose. Hell, Dorothy, I would have said. You're canned.

There stood Dorothy, burdened with the customary pad and pencil. In the past two years I'd had to fire four people. One of them, a small blonde, had immediately slumped back in her chair. "My father is sick," she said. "Did you know that? How can you do this when my father is so sick?"

Dorothy was no amateur in life. She must have seen what was coming, because she refused to take a seat. Perhaps I was tapping the envelope. She just leaned back against the door and crossed her arms. Her expression was cynical, weary, unfriendly.

"I'm truly sorry, Dorothy," I began. "But the economy, you realize. There have been cutbacks all around. I will certainly give you a reference. Have them write directly to me."

"Yes," she said and held out her hand.

I gave her the envelope, and she said nothing further but immediately left the room, closing the door quietly behind her.

Only once before had it been that easy. A man had stood in Dorothy's spot and said some words not clearly heard. "What?" I had asked. But he only shook his head and left.

I had delayed my lunch. I was eating my sandwich when Malverne, the reception area office manager, knocked on my door. "Gone," she announced. "Dorothy left. She just put on her coat, said so long, and walked out."

"So?" I tasted lettuce, the bitter ends of roast beef.

"It's her office." Malverne's cheeks were reddened by the pain of holding back. "She didn't clean out her office. And that room is being borrowed by Fiscal this very afternoon."

I felt the blame. Dorothy was in my department. I could have ordered Malverne to clean out the office. The old fox had expected that, hoped to forestall it by complaints.

"Get a carton," I said. "Find a carton somewhere. We'll empty into it. Dorothy will probably come back to get her things."

After I finished eating, I walked down the corridor to Dorothy's office. She had abandoned ship. Papers on her desk from the morning's assignment. Pen uncapped and two sharpened pencils near the lamp.

Malverne was sly. The carton was already by the desk. Malverne was not. I stacked the papers from the top of the desk into the In basket. Work that I would assign to someone else. This was going to be simple. Three of the drawers were stuffed with supplies, nothing else. I bequeathed them to Fiscal. I had only to clean out the top side drawer—the usual personal junk. Towards the back of the drawer a blue spiral notebook, not office issue. I opened the notebook to the first page—*My Life Story!* Now that I would save for later.

Not enough in the desk to require a carton. I slid what there was into a large manila envelope and labeled it *Dorothy.* I took the envelope back to my office and put it on the shelf behind the desk.

I stiffened my back and went home. "I slit a throat today," I told my husband.

"It's often a question of retrenchment," my husband said. "You have to swing with them." He shook his head. "You have to swing with them."

"My education was not just in the school of life," my father wrote me. "I was for many years a night school student. But I worked through the hardest times. For instance when I worked for Kulmisca. I went one day into Mrs. Kulmisca's office, thinking in my mind that of all the ways, the open confrontation was the best. I was promised a summer job, a full-time summer job. Now to face no summer job and the loss of even the few hours I was paid. Mrs. Kulmisca, I said, I fail to understand. No, that is not the best way to put it. I understand too well. I have been found to be dangerous. I will never tell. Didn't I say that I will never tell? I understand, Mrs. Kulmisca, that you do not know me so well, but I will never tell. My word is enough. I have an understanding with nature—no, hear me out. I grew up on a farm. Farm as it was. Not farm as it is. It was outdoors, there was so little machinery. Mrs. Kulmisca, I can be trusted. Didn't I say that I would not tell?"

*   *   *

The girl on the flying trapeze went back to work. What was I going to do? I was going to open that notebook. *My Life Story!* Who could pass that up? A chance at someone's life. Afterwards, I might joke about it with Arthur. "An addition to my voyeuristic past," I would say. "The past of a peeker and a pryer."

Twice I had read secret diaries. A friend trusted me. The diary was always on top of his dresser. I read it, parts of it.

But Dorothy was different. I didn't really know Dorothy. I took the notebook from the envelope. Not a lined notebook, an artist's notebook. I flipped the pages, a bunch of circles and lines. I concentrated.

I turned to the first page. Dorothy had drawn three circles positioned to form a triangle with lines ending in arrows connecting each circle. The lines were so fine and sharp that she must have drawn them with a mechanical pencil.

The top circle was labeled Me, the one on the left was Mama, and at the right, Papa. She was certainly beginning at the beginning—the place where you say I was born in a little log cabin.

An Artist's View of Life! An Artist Looks at Life! My Life as an Artist!

Her life, my life. I hunted in my desk for my clear plastic meter ruler. I used it to measure Dorothy's lines. Each line was exactly fifty millimeters. I took a piece of paper from my wooden memo box. Using the ruler I drew my first line and then the circle freehand. Hers were better. The point of my number two pencil dulled quickly. I sharpened the pencil for the next try, one line, resharpened the pencil for the circle, next line, resharpened.

In my top circle I printed Me, to the left Papa, on the right Mama. Was Dorothy an only child? Did my brother count? He had gone, disappeared into dark ways, a pioneer in misery. I mourn for him, my father had said. But it's like he never was.

Now the setup of my family tree wasn't exactly Dorothy's. Instinctively I had done the reverse. Mama second in line. Did it matter who came first? Facts were facts. She didn't seem to be around all that often. Faulty memory, perhaps. There I was in Union Station, a little girl of five or six, and bawling my eyes out as Mama's back retreated from me. I called out, I begged. I was held back by an aunt who pinned my arms tightly. In the distortions of childhood, Mama might have been going nowhere, Mama might have left me to purchase tickets, I might have been accompanying her. There might not have been a lover waiting for her on the other side of the pillar.

I turned the next page. Dorothy had drawn three large circles. Beauties those were—no freehand scrawl of mine would come close. I was either going to do this properly or not at all. I dialed Malverne on the intercom. "Are you going out for lunch?" I asked.

Her hesitation was deliberate, but then she was aware that if she said no, I would expect to see her sitting there with sandwich and waxed paper and cartons. "Yes," she said. "Yes, I am."

"Would you mind," I said, "taking a few extra minutes and stopping across the street at the office supply store and buying me a compass."

"What?"

"Ask the man," I said testily, "for a compass for making circles."

*   *   *

I had felt the tiny holes in the paper where Dorothy had placed the point of her compass to make the three circles. She used the same names on each circle, but the order differed. Ann, Mary, Sue, John, Dorothy, Dick. Mary, Dorothy, John, Sue, Ann, Dick. John, Ann, Dorothy, Sue, Dick, Mary. Was she saying that the sequence did not matter in first circles? No necessity for boy, girl, boy, girl.

I needn't change the names for my circles, those names would do—I just added my own. Weren't all children's names alike? I was certain that those people had existed for me, that we had joined hands and moved in a clock-wise motion—first John then Ann then Sue then Dick then Mary then I. Playing our games with no self-consciousness, no giggling, just a chant culminating in the command, "All fall down!"

I had Malverne's compass. Brittle yellow plastic instead of metal. I believed that she must have selected that one on purpose. As if perhaps she might not be repaid for the metal one. Nevertheless, the yellow one did just as well, made circles of the proper circumference for my small sheets of paper and my sharpened pencils.

My father called me on the telephone. "I was in construction at the time," he said. "Now maybe I'm mistaken, but I never saw a mansion or say a really big house downed by a tornado. Tornadoes go a lot to developments, to mobile homes, whipping through poor folks like the caress of God. There was some loss of life. The tornado came down about six in the morning. It took the back wall of the Lancelot Apartment complex. Made stage sets of the place. Driving by and looking, those rooms seemed less than life-size. The police came and yelled, You all get out of there. We waited until they had gone away, sirens blasting good morning, and then we went right back in to sign up the customers."

On Dorothy's next page were two interlocking circles. So we've gone into our group phase, have we? All the names of the first circle were repeated, with a few additions, but now all the girls were on one circle and the boys on the other. Ann, Mary, Sue, Cele, Audrey, Dorothy. The circles looped, and John, Dick, Roger, Yale, Frederick were in the second circle. A lot of the same names. This girl had really stable relationships. Didn't she ever move? Jesus, my mother used to say, I sign up for ballroom and tap at Arthur Murray, canasta at the Legion hall, and it's covered wagon time again.

"Can you remember your childhood friends?" I asked my husband that evening.

He was reading, thinking, he was annoyed.

"What's that?" he said.

But he had heard, and he answered. "Some. I remember some. It depends. I remember a bully named Christopher."

I did not remember a bully named Christopher. There was of course the prettiest circle, led by a girl admired for the smallness of her ankles, for the slimness of her wrists. I never belonged to that circle.

On my paper I drew my own circles. Sally, Edith, Roberta, Elizabeth, Barbara. They would have to cross with the circle of Eugene, Nelson, who was my cousin, and Steven. I had no more names. I spaced mine wider, measuring so that they were evenly placed around the circle.

Next came four lines ending with arrows, each line fifty millimeters long, one circle at each corner. Dorothy was lower left and above was Frederick. Audrey and Yale occupied the other circles. I knew that configuration. I placed myself at lower left, above was Steven, and at the opposite ends were Elizabeth and Eugene. I wore purple lipstick that year. You stay out one more time, my father had said, and you're going to have to learn to walk all over again. Steven and I behaved, as did Elizabeth, whose hair was black, and Eugene. We paired in that season and moved together.

"Do you remember your first love?" I asked my husband.

"My first love," my husband said savagely, "occurred in Westfield one Thursday night. You remember Westfield?"

"No more," I said. "I do not wish to hear about those adventures."

Dorothy had drawn a line seventy-five millimeters long exactly parallel to the bottom edge of the page. At each end was a circle, one labeled Frederick and the other Dorothy. They'd ditched the others, I realized. I measured my line and printed my name in one circle and Eugene in the other. Steven had gone off at once with someone else. What do you expect? he had said. I never asked for any of this, he had said. So when I went after Eugene, I knew what I was doing. But Elizabeth? I had some memory of Elizabeth in disorder, of Elizabeth running.

On the next page the triangle of circles reappeared. The top circle labeled Baby, and the others Mama and Papa. I did the same.

There were noises from Fiscal, the sound of their machines, the complicity of Malverne's laughter. I must temporarily stop. So I put aside my artistic endeavors, my sheaf of memo paper, my pencil, my yellow compass. I had to

face my work. There was a report due the next day that I
had not yet begun. After all, I collected a salary. Also,
there was a meeting at which I must speak.

I had lunch with Arthur that day, and twice I started to
mention the notebook, but I did not. We spoke about our
reports.

"Get on the good side of clerical," my father wrote.
"They can fry you. For instance the one at Lonsberg's.
Are you Jewish? she says to me the first day. You look
like a Hebrew. Well, never mind. Don't answer, if you
don't want. Now Mr. Lonsberg is a fine one, she says.
He is the soul of religiosity. Observant. There's a list of
holidays, I know them all. From Rosh Hodesh to Sukkoth.
Days, hours, a fascinating choice. But what I'm getting
at, she says, is that you can be here, you see, and Mr.
Lonsberg isn't. To be at work when the boss isn't is a
picnic. Now if you're like me—a Catholic. Observant. So
I get off all my own days. The combination is such that I
find to my heart's content a perfect set of circumstances.

"You'd think from that she's a honey," my father
wrote. "One month later she says to me, Mr. Lonsberg
says go. Yes, she says, he always leaves the telling to me.
Mr. Lonsberg checked, and there is no Church of the
Fifteenth Pentecostal. Oh, I am so disappointed in you.
The very golden goose you have overdone."

Two days later I was able to return to Dorothy's notebook at the place where I had stopped. Dorothy had
drawn a vertical line sixty millimeters long with her name
at the bottom and two circles forming a V shape at the
top. Frederick was printed in one circle, and James in the
other.

Could we part here? Should I label her slut as my mother would have said? She with her lover.

So I drew my line, the circles to form a V, and printed my Jonathan and my Norrel. I could draw one for my husband, couldn't I? A similar line with God knew how many circles for names.

I'm no dreamer. I knew the life of hard knocks. I could read the cards dealt for our Dorothy. The husband gone. Now would come the line with more circles—not just two. I'd bet a reasonable sum that James would not last. The divorced middle-aged woman, the child. Good-bye James.

On the following page was a circle—just one large circle. I was disappointed. Dorothy had been fired too soon. She didn't have time to finish. I put the notebook back into the envelope. My own sheets were paper-clipped and placed in my middle desk drawer.

I went home to spend the evening with my husband. But he had left a message on our answering machine. He was working late. He would not be home for dinner. So I ate with our son, who was fourteen.

In the morning I checked my telephone file at work. Dorothy's home number was still there. Sometimes people had to be called on weekends, when there was a rush job. It was ten o'clock when I dialed her number. She answered almost at once. That was a bad sign, she was still out of work. I recognized her expectant tone of voice.

I identified myself.

"Yes?" she said, her voice becoming cool at once.

"When you left," I said, "there were some things— some personal items in your desk. I didn't know what you wanted done with them."

"Toss," Dorothy said.

"You left a notebook," I said.

"Good-bye," Dorothy said.

She had hung up. That was not the way to behave if you wanted a reference. I picked up the manila envelope. "Toss," I said and threw it in the wastebasket.

Arthur took me out for drinks. I spoke to him about Dorothy and the notebook. Arthur thought it was very funny. "My life as a circle," he said.

"I had midnight supper with Lana," my father said on the telephone. "Never drop a contact. They say, she told me, that the factory is sold. Sold, I said. To whom? How? It was not in the papers. Lana smiled. Everything is not in the papers, she said. Powerful people can keep facts out. The factory is a privately held business. The stock in the family. Have a gin and tonic, she said. Cooling. At least you have Unemployment. Not me, I said. I'm staying. It's worse when they push, she said. Push? I asked. Oh yes, she said. They can make you leave. Annoyances. Believe me it can be done. Then you leave and you have nothing. There is no way they will push me out, I said. I can stand up to anything."

I took a sheet of paper and drew one large freehand circle. The circle filled the entire sheet, and in the middle I printed ME. I pinned the paper on my bulletin board. According to my calendar, I had a two o'clock meeting, a three o'clock meeting, and a four o'clock meeting.

"Never," my father said, whispering into the answering machine, "never let anything get between you and success."

Piers the Imposter

~~~~~~~~

My new boy friend is named Alexander. He is a dumpling of a man. We have reached the point in our relationship where we have begun to speak our histories. So far I've limited mine—I've been selective. But when we are alone, some evening, some night, I shall slip, I know. I shall lapse into Ira's adventure. Starting with the core of the tale, without losing its essence, I rethink it. I recall the times I've told the tale to lovers, to husbands, to groups at parties, and to half strangers on airplanes. I realize that I have begun it at different points, sometimes when Ira assumes the new identity, sometimes starting with the purchase of the house by the lake, sometimes with an explanation of our lives. My explanations are a widening pool.

Alexander, I will say, have some coffee, have a brandy, let me tempt you with a lemon-scented pastry. My brother Ira, I will add, had an adventure, a few perfect moments.

The point where an adventure begins is not easily determined. Life slides back and forth. I have loved various people, some worthy, some lacking in grace. I'll outfit no one with blame.

Ira and I and the family we came from lived a life that was slovenly, cluttered, lunatic. I would have said it then, I say it now. I was age fourteen, and my nature was not melancholy. Our mother ran a business from the ground-floor rooms of our house. She was Stella of Stella's Fashions—For the Large Woman. Among the lies I used to tell is that everything would have been different if our father had not died. How could a man that peripheral to our daily lives have changed anything? I think of friends who have lost their fathers. The casual dying of American fathers must be endemic. I can't speak for those friends, though. Perhaps their lives would have been different.

We lived in a dusty, narrow house off Mosholu Parkway in the Bronx, on the very edges of commercial zoning. Around us were apartment houses, people looked down on us in our yard, staring, I believe, from darkened windows, and counting the leaves of our trees. Our mother had a reputation that spread from gossip—for I don't believe she ever advertised. But women found her, heavy Russian-style women, fur-wrapped gryphons traveling from distant boroughs—coming for her drapes, her tucks, her folds. She was not cheap. The customers arrived mostly in long black cars, and their drivers would pace up and down in front of the house.

The business claimed the three best rooms of the house. All that was left to us downstairs was the kitchen and the enclosed back porch. The house had a bad smell. It was no more than the stench of women whitened with talcum spreading the luxuriant odors of their estrous cycles. Our mother herself sprayed the rooms with heavy perfumes. At night the heat sizzled at all times from radiators. Our mucous membranes withered, and our lungs exploded in catarrh. In good times, two old women chatting to each other in Polish came to help, working their Singers behind a curtain. No, no, Mother would shriek at them. Where are your eyes? Fix it, you idiots!

Think now of my dressmaker mother. Bolts of material cushioning her walls. From scarlet to midnight blue, from rugs of velvet deep as molasses to finely veined silks. This stitcher of clothes never made me a dress. I swear that. She never took up needle and thread for us.

All right, I take away the blame. She was on her knees most of the day batting her eyes up at her clients. On the other hand, let me explain about zippers that caught the flesh, brass pins that nicked the knees, pointed-tipped scissors pricking inward where bellies rested loop on loop.

Sometimes the women would weep standing in the fitting room like apostates in thick pink corset satin.

I was a brilliant child. I say this without shame. My I.Q. was often tested. I was a fierce and ugly competitor. I was a striver and where did it get me? All those Best Papers. Ira was smart but lackadaisical. He spent his days playing baseball in Van Cortlandt Park. The worst time was when I was eight and skipped a grade. That put me in Ira's class. He couldn't stand that. It took him two years, but when he was eleven they finally skipped him.

I make our mother sound like a widow living in that house with the support of her children on her back. But at the time this adventure begins she was married to our father, a former wartime sweetheart. There is nothing unusual in the marriage of my mother and my father. Their life was full of cowardices, omissions, bleating complaints. My father handled that by acquiring an

American occupation. He traveled. Any advertisement that promised—*Be able to leave at a moment's notice*—he answered.

When he was successful he made grand gestures. He bought me when I was ten years old a set of riding clothes—jodhpurs, ankle-high leather boots, a jacket, the right hat. When I put on those clothes I could hardly see my trembling reflection in the mirror. I developed dreams of sweat before my time. One year he gave Ira a complete American Flyer train.

The house by the lake, like the riding clothes or the American Flyer train, was not given in lieu of love. Not at all. Our father loved us, there are different frequencies of love. These gifts were part of his nature—he gave them whenever he could. Day-to-day life was hard for him. I can't trace his past enough to explain. I can't tell you what I don't know. His name was Edward, and he was the last son of six children.

The spring I turned fourteen my father had a good year. He had been assigned the Maritime Provinces as his territory. On his way home he bought us the house by the lake.

Can't you guess the reaction of Stella of Stella's Fashions? She swore that she would have no part of it. Keep it, she said. Our father was home, and he wooed her, slowly, tactfully. And Mother began to tell her customers that she was going up to her summer place. And that July we packed suitcases and boxes and filled the back of the station wagon belonging to Stella's Fashions.

Mother would do the driving. Me, me, me, she shouted. He's left me with everything to do. The two of you will behave. Bad enough we have hours on the road—a woman and two children. I closed my eyes, riding most of the trip that way. It was the sensation of leaving that I was cherishing. The destination was not important.

When we arrived, the house rose up in front of us, a small grey palace. We gasped, and we rushed at it like raiders. My father had named the house like a boat. *The Stella* was done in red and yellow scrolls on a sign that hung from two short chains in the middle of the porch roof.

The house was the product of summer architect Miller Trumbell, circa 1920. A period piece with too many rooms for us. We were city children. We swam, we walked the beach, we were bored within the week. We whined to go home, we raged against peace and quiet. The mosquitoes are killing me, Ira said. Their life replenished from his shoulders. The calamine kid, my father called him. I blistered my chest that first week. My body, I believed, responding to the environment, the sand, the lack of company. My red rose, my father said.

There we sat in an original Miller Trumbell. We didn't even know enough to put up the blue awnings packed away in the cellar. What was happening with Stella of Stella's Fashions? She loved the house by the lake. Every morning she would bind her hair in a silk scarf, oil her body, and carry an old blue blanket down to the sand. That we knew no one, that we spoke to no one, didn't bother her. Let the goyim be, she said. She hummed to herself, stretched out on her blanket, and with her hand made temporary gashes in the sand.

This was the only summer our father ever spent in that house. I try to remember him walking on the beach, bathing in the water, urging us to come along. But I am not certain it is true. In October he died. Mother received the telephone call. The will was unexpected. My father was not the kind of man who makes a will. Almost all of his worldly goods, he left to his beloved wife Stella. He gave everything to our mother except the summer house at the lake. That he left equally to Ira and to me.

Our mother didn't seem to mind. Why should I? she said. What's yours is mine. But she had to get in those little digs. Sweethearts, she'd say, I've painted your inheritance with a swell coat of all-weather white. From a bottle of suntan lotion, I've paid your taxes.

Through everything I remained the perfect, the terrific student. Two of my teachers told my mother that I should go to a private school. They said that as much as they could give me I deserved more. They tried to persuade her, but she would have none of it. Was she jealous? She was the second of four sisters. Fools—every one of them, she said. We had to take her word for that, because by the time we were born she was not talking to those sisters. Who needs them? she said. I could have gone on and become a real designer, she said. We believed her. Her parents could see no sense in educating her further. On our mother's side the heritage is one of peddlers. There was no pretense of scholars, no students of the Talmud, no rabbis.

Our father's side is more of a mystery, although we knew our grandfather. He was a man who lived with us for three years until he married again. He slept in Ira's room. The day he left, our mother spat in his direction. An old man, she said, should at least be faithful to a memory—fifty-three years married, and it's gone just like that.

This grandfather used to read to us tales. It was from him that we first heard about *The Three Princes of Serendip*. I consider this an important story, he said. Serendipity, Grandfather said, is the moving force in our family.

Grandfather was a naturalist. And famous, Grandfather

said, a famous naturalist. Sometimes he said that he had been at the Universität at Berne or the Universität at Stalzbourg or even the Polytech at Moscovy.

Our grandfather's name was to be found nowhere. Not in any university catalogue. One day, wandering through the section of the library given over to Germanic languages, Ira pulled down a book. Drawn to it, he said later, by the serpentine vine printed on the spine. It was in the pages of that book that Ira found grandfather's name. He had existed.

The adventure is coming closer. A return to the house by the lake became a goal as diligently pursued as any errant thread. We will go, Mother said. She alternated between commander or coaxer or wheedler or widow. I am your bread and butter, she would declare.

Ira went out day after day in search of summer employment, a hopeless task for any unskilled child of small build with black wavy hair and cautious voice.

And the conversation continued.

"I'm not going back to the lake," Ira said. It was the summer after our father died. "I'm going to stay in the city and get a job."

"You?" our mother said. "You? Who will hire you—I want to know? A pipsqueak like you?"

"A whole summer in that place will kill me," Ira said.

"You'll love it," Mother said, her voice at its flirtatious best.

While Ira was having his adventure, was I blind and dumb? Was the air more pungent? Did I lick the salt from my lips? I had begun to read romances where lovers pressed vanilla kisses on closed paper lips. But of Ira's adventure, I never knew, I never guessed. He burned with deceit. I marked only the passing of some chimera.

We went to the lake the next year too—all of us. It was the last time for Ira. But Mother and I kept going back every summer until I left home. Afterwards, Mother continued to go alone to the lake. She left that house to Ira and me in her will when she died. Her new lawyer hadn't realized that she couldn't leave us the house. It was ours already.

What irritates? Sometimes the smallest burdens. I was the one responsible for arranging the rentals for the summer house. Ira was quick to take his share of the money—but I did the work. It was geographic, you see. Ira lived in Los Angeles. I lived in New York City. Then came the year when I was getting my divorce. I had no energy to spare. I turned the summer house over to an agency. They handled everything, the taxes, the advertising, the cleaning up after tenants.

One day second homes were suddenly in boom times. The lake had changed, built up, become fashionable. We had an offer for the house. I telephoned Ira with news of the prospective buyer. I could hear his wife's voice in the background. "What does she want?" she kept saying.

"Fantastic news," Ira said. "God, can we use the money. Sell—don't hesitate—sell."

The offer was accepted. I wrote to Ira. Did he want anything from the house? Any mementos? He called me. What was I to think? I don't believe that my reaction was unusual. He wanted a suitcase. I didn't remember the suitcase. It used to be on the top shelf of the closet under the stairs. Be careful, he said, it's very heavy.

A suitcase? My brother wanted an old suitcase. What came to me was that something of our father's was there, something concealed, a treasure not to be shared with me. Perhaps news of the sale had jolted Ira's memory—made him remember. Never mind that some tenant might have walked off with the suitcase. There was urgency in Ira's voice. Yes, I definitely had heard urgency.

On Friday I drove to the house directly from my office. I went at once to the closet. It was a dark closet, smelling of cozy dampness. The suitcase was on the top shelf, a boxy rectangle, canvas covered and yellowed from coats of varnish, with a girdle of three green stripes.

I was dignified at first. I dragged the suitcase into the sunroom. It wasn't locked, and it was empty. Ira had said it was empty. I patted the brown cloth lining and, finding one corner loose, I ripped it. It came away easily, bits of glue like rough chunks of amber hanging onto the threads. It was a roller-coaster then. I plunged into the elasticized pockets, tore the stitching, making terrible cuts in my palm. Under the lining was a thin layer of cotton batting still startlingly white. I grabbed at it, and the cotton burst forth in tiny tutus of gauze. The suitcase, though, retained its integrity, its shape. That's when I went into the kitchen and found the cleaver. Holding it like an axe, I chopped.

The suitcase cannot be located, I wrote to Ira. The house was sold. Ira said he would fly in for the closing. He said he had other business in the city, but I knew that was a lie. His wife had put him up to it, I was certain. Go yourself, she must have said, see it for yourself. As if I would do anything—as if it weren't all down in black and white.

The actual business of the sale went quickly. It was concluded in the city. The new owners were represented by a lawyer. Afterwards Ira and I were in high spirits. I hugged my brother. "Look at you," I said, "all California—the hair, the clothes. Come back to my apartment and we'll celebrate."

"Let's go," Ira said.

We stopped at a small store I knew and bought chilled wine, thin slices of Scotch smoked salmon, curves of ripe Brie, crisp bread, and more fruit than we could eat. In my apartment I spread the food before us on the low glass-topped coffee table. We feasted and were happy. I poured more wine into Ira's glass. He was relaxed. I thought he seemed younger, more brotherly.

I was careful. "Sorry about the suitcase," I said.

Ira waved his hand. "Nothing," he said. "Just a whim."

"But you wanted it—and it was gone. I don't really remember that suitcase. Was it yours? One that you used?"

Ira laughed. "It belonged to Piers Angell."

"Who?"

"I've told you," Ira said. "Surely, I've told you?"

"No."

"Me," Ira said. "I was Piers Angell." Ira leaned back in his chair, tilting the wineglass towards his lips. He smiled at me. "A toast," he said, "to the brief life of Piers Angell."

This is the adventure of Piers. These are Ira's words:

I am not ever to be thought of as a boy of boldness and daring, although I have a tested I.Q. of 170. I lived my childhood in a daze, spent it with trains and Meccano sets, kept stocks of chemicals, had secret thoughts of destructive devices. I was a popular boy, I had friends, I had girls. I had many dreams formed from movies and magazines and stories.

Piers was born the summer after my father died. What I wanted can be fully understood. I wanted to emigrate, I wanted to go into exile, I was willing to impersonate a pilgrim. I was however a boy, not a warrior. I didn't want to go away to the summer house by the lake. Keep your lakes—I'll stay in the confines of washbasins. I wanted independence. You have a heart of steel, Mother said.

Was summer life different from winter life? We were a family without set routines, our days moved by the demands of trade, we ate as we could. I imagined my escape every night. By day my lack of cunning was apparent. I did as I was told. I swam, I roamed the area. Do anything, Mother would say. Only leave me alone.

I stalked the beach. The beach itself curves, and two houses are visible to us from the left, but the bend of sand hides one—and that is the one that matters. It was a big white Victorian with green cloth awnings, a steamship of a house, a half-mile away. The house belonged to the Rampels.

Picture me, a boy of sixteen, spending his afternoons in town at a store near the movie theater—ice cream, sodas, odds and ends. I would sit there in a corner booth, a scarred, mutilated booth covered with initials of love.

Think of old Mrs. Rampel—old to me anyway—grey hair, stiff walk, old-fashioned manners. I saw her one day, knew who she was when the younger woman with her, a summer visitor, spoke to her. The two women escaping from the sun to sit near me in that store, to sip sodas, to talk. Did they look at me? Did they see me? I was nothing to them.

All summer people look alike. The postman, indifferent to our identity, dropped our mail into the wicker basket attached by a slender nail to the porch railing. The mail seldom varied—advertisements from local stores, glossy postcards from Mother's best customers spending their Augusts by larger lakes with warmer weather, and the occasional plea from a city relative. When we remembered, we emptied the wicker basket.

I was the one who saw the envelope. The blue envelope—caught between a postcard and a hardware sale circular—was as thick as a pencil. It was not our letter. The sender was Mrs. N. Rampel—outgoing mail intended for San Francisco—given to the postman. The letter had traveled only as far as our house. I held the envelope between thumb and forefinger, made a cave of it, the paper flap popped up. The glue had been dampened by a parched tongue.

Dear Friend—began the letter. I sighed. Much time had passed between letters, but the weather was fine, the lake was calm, and all were in good health. Then suddenly the tone of the letter changed. A sadness entered, regrets. Mrs. Rampel was growing older—and thought again of her brother, her poor brother who had died young. Every year she invited his son to the lake. Her nephew. Perhaps this year he would come and not disappoint her. The only son of her dead brother—his namesake. Piers Angell.

You assume that it is hard to be an imposter, beyond the ken of a boy. I say it is easy. I say that identity is casually worn. And for me to become Piers Angell was no more than the assemblage of information. I read that letter from *Dear Friend* to its closing *Your Friend*. Bit by bit I gleaned what I needed. The nephew's name was Piers Angell. He lived in Wyoming. His father was dead. He lived with his mother and her second husband. He was fifteen. He was interested in nature and had requested a field book about flora and fauna of the Northwest for his most recent birthday. He and his mother had last visited Mrs. Rampel in New York City the winter Piers was ten. The invited guest who never arrived, whose room was prepared, whose sad arrival was expected on the second Monday in August.

Perhaps it was madness. The truth is that I did not consider the dangers. I decided just like that. Piers had never come before. Why shouldn't he arrive now? Did I even think of appearance? That Piers might be blond, that he might look nothing like a boy descended from peddlers and real naturalists. No, not for a moment. All I regretted was that I must be fifteen. I was sixteen. I was about to lose a year.

The details, the logistics were amazingly simple. I packed most of my clothes in one of the suitcases that our father had left in the house, a huge suitcase with three green stripes. On Mondays the train from the city arrived at one o'clock. I could then reasonably show up at the Rampels' somewhere between one-thirty and a quarter to two. I combed my hair, put on clean pants and a plaid shirt that I had ironed.

I had ordered one of the town taxis to pick me up at the intersection of Meadow Way and Lakeside Road just past the Shell station. I dragged the suitcase through the jimsonweed and up the embankment behind our house to the road and began to walk to my rendezvous. The suitcase was heavy, and I was sweating when I reached my destination. It was all right. I looked as if I had spent the day on trains. The man who drove the taxi didn't care where he took me. Summer people were all strange. The charge was the same—a flat rate for less than five miles.

The maid answered the door. Mrs. Rampel was called.

"Piers?" she said.

"Yes ma'am."

It began so easily. My new aunt, her arm around my shoulders, guiding me through the large dining room and out onto the porch where lunch was served. Several strangers smiled at me.

"Look," my aunt said, "who has arrived! It's Piers."

I had never imagined people in the house. I had seen only Mrs. Rampel and the friend, and once a man who I had thought was probably Mr. Rampel walking down the beach near the house.

That same man now stood up and held out his hand. "Good to have you here, Piers."

"Yes sir," I said and shook hands.

Everyone smiled at me. I was running on sheer child's nerve. A song of introductions began. I nodded, I whispered, my hand was damp.

"The boy must be hungry," said my uncle.

"Of course," my aunt said.

Later I learned from notes and envelopes that my uncle was named Nathaniel and my aunt was Elsa. Wyoming proved no problem. From a bookcase in the sunroom I took an encyclopedia volume labeled *Vascu–Zygote* up to my room.

But that first afternoon I put on my swimming trunks and went for a trial walk down the beach to where my mother sat on the sand.

"Hello," I called.

Mother looked up and squinted into the light. "Hot dogs," she said, "in the fridge."

"Right," I said. "For later."

I turned around and headed back to the Rampels'. Could I tell my mother that my stomach was full of broiled fish, tomatoes, fresh bread, peaches in wine? I did a cartwheel. My new summer life had begun.

At intervals I offered the Rampels items acquired from the encyclopedia—where to pick the best specimens of *Castilleja linariasefolia* or a discussion of sage grouse. I even walked down the stairs singing *Whoopee ti yi yo, git along little dogies, for you know Wyoming will be your new home.*

There was nothing that I wouldn't do for authenticity.

The Rampel house shut up every evening at eleven. I established a routine. Twenty minutes after the house grew quiet, I left by the front door. I always wore my swimming trunks. I would run down the beach to *our* house. I'm getting into condition for hockey, I would say. Every night I slept in my own bed.

Once Mother inquired, "Didn't you eat anything today?"

I learned then to remove what I considered to be my day's food from the refrigerator and put it into a paper bag. The bags I buried in the sand by the road. I lived by the rigors of deception, the thoughtful reply, the pause.

Mornings, I made enough noise to be told to cut the racket, then, having firmly established my presence, I would run back down the beach, stopping just before I reached the Rampel house to get wet in the lake.

If anyone in the Rampel house had ever checked my room at night and found me absent, it was never mentioned. Of course I left the bed rumpled. My clothes were washed and ironed in the Rampel house. I had never looked better. I even put on some weight.

I overheard Aunt Elsa remarking to her husband one evening, "He looks nothing like Brother—nothing at all."

"Not in appearance," her husband said, "but he has your brother's spirit."

"Yes," Aunt Elsa said, "yes, the spirit is there."

I believed that I was safe for the summer, but at the end of two weeks Aunt Elsa suddenly asked me which train I was scheduled to take. The invitation to Piers had been for two weeks. There would be new guests arriving.

"But next summer," Aunt Elsa said, "would you like to come for an entire month? Uncle Nathaniel and I would be pleased to have you here."

"Yes ma'am," I said.

Aunt Elsa put me down on her calendar for the month of August.

The problem was that *we* were not to leave the lake for another ten days. Where could I hide? I was now known, I would be seen, I would be recognized. The first night after Piers, bound for Wyoming, had departed from the Rampels', I developed a great pain. I moaned, refused to leave the house, could not be coaxed into the sunlight. The doctor who was called found nothing wrong. Summer doctor, my mother said. She became worried. We closed up the house and went back to the city. I recovered.

I planned the next summer carefully. I offered no resistance to the idea of going to the house by the lake in August. Growing up at last, Mother said. The big shot! On the first of August, I took my suitcase and a large box of chocolates carried from the city and rang the doorbell of the Rampel house. Piers had returned for the last time.

That was Ira's adventure. What a wonderful time he must have had—the meals, the servants, the cool Protestant elegance. And just imagine the strength of character needed to keep such a secret all to yourself. I personally couldn't have done it. I bet you couldn't either, Alexander. You would have spilled the beans.

I know what you are thinking. I look at your bull-shaped head. I can interpret your snorting snickers. The adolescent boy and girl rebelling against the domineering mother. What a classic situation! Then the boy escapes into fantasy. That's what you are thinking, and you are welcome to your thoughts, mister. If Ira says it happened, then it happened. I try to remember what I was like, what Ira was like. Who behaved right, who behaved badly.

When did I begin staying away? I knew that I was supposed to be the devoted daughter, like it had been arranged, like Bette Davis in that movie. But I never jumped into that role. Even when Mother, now putting on weight, hurt her ankle, I forced her to hire a stranger to fetch and carry. Then that summer when I became pregnant, I drove to the house by the lake just to tell her. "What?" my mother said. "What?" But I ran back to the car, to the man waiting for me in the car.

If I had known, though, if Ira had told me about the possibilities of a secret life that altered everything, that could make you be polite and kind the way he was those last years before he went away, perhaps I wouldn't have had to leave that old woman sitting alone in the sand, kicking and screaming.

Bette Pesetsky was born in Milwaukee, Wisconsin, and educated in the midwest. A graduate of Washington University in St. Louis, she received an M.F.A. from the University of Iowa Writers Workshop. Recipient of a National Endowment for the Arts Grant, she is the author of three novels and one earlier collection of short stories. Her stories have appeared in *Paris Review, Vogue, The New Yorker, Ontario Review, Vanity Fair,* and other magazines. Ms. Pesetsky is married to a professor of anatomy, has one son, and lives in upstate New York.